Eddie's Blue-Winged Dragon

EDDIE'S Blue-Winged Dragon

C. S. ADLER

G. P. PUTNAM'S SONS
NEW YORK

ACKNOWLEDGMENT:

With many thanks to Karin Kowalchyk, Vice President Foundation, and Nancy Gorman, Speech Pathologist of the Cerebral Palsy Center for the Disabled, for their willing cooperation and help in educating me and checking the material on cerebral palsy in this book.

Thanks also to Pauline Kraft for sharing grandchildren stories that helped me in depicting Mina.

Published simultaneously in Canada.
Book design by Gunta Alexander
Printed in the United States of America
First impression.

Library of Congress Cataloging-in-Publication Data
Adler, C. S. (Carole S.) Eddie's blue-winged dragon /
C. S. Adler. p. cm. Summary: A sixth-grader with
cerebral palsy becomes the owner of a
brass dragon which helps him out in some of
the battles he faces due to his handicap.
ISBN 0-399-21535-2 [1. Cerebral palsy—Fiction.
2. Physically handicapped—Fiction.
3. Dragons—Fiction.] I. Title PZ7.A26145Ed 1988
[Fic]—dc19 87-25649 CIP AC

In memory of our beloved son,

Clifford Paul Adler

He stood tall in the world, and many
looked up to him, for he was a giving man.
He knew how to laugh.
He was a high-energy yea sayer to life.
In his short thirty-three years,
he packed a long lifetime of accomplishments.
He will be remembered.

Contents

I

Money for the Birthday Present

Eddie considered hiding the five dollars in his orthopedic shoes, but why should he? He had nothing to be afraid of. He was just a regular kid going to a regular school now. He shoved the hateful brown clunkers under his bed, pocketed the money and set off for the bus stop in his sneakers.

After school today, he was going to buy his little sister, Mina, a present for her sixth birthday. It was something she really wanted for a change. In fact, she'd clapped her hands in delight when she'd spotted the green ceramic elf in the window of The Treasure Shop while they'd waited for Eddie's friend, Gary, to finish sweeping up inside.

"You *like* that?" Eddie had asked her doubtfully when he saw where she was looking.

"He's the one in my story book," Mina had said.

Then he's yours, Eddie had thought immediately.

He was feeling great as he shoved open the heavy glass door of the school and began lurching down the empty hall toward his sixth grade classroom. He felt great until he got to the corner. Then he saw Darrin waiting there like a muscular spider for a fly. Guessing he was likely to be the fly, Eddie put on a smile and said, "Hi. You here for wrestling practice?"

Darrin fixed Eddie with blue needle eyes and drawled, "Well, look who's here. Hey, Richard, Mack, look who got to school early." A wide grin squared off Darrin's meaty face. His hood friends walled up the corridor behind him. The gym door was locked. So they weren't here to wrestle.

It was either try to slip past them or retreat to the front door and hope somebody, a teacher maybe, would be coming in early. "Oops," Eddie said. "Forgot something." He turned fast, but before he could take a step, Darrin's thick arm wrapped around Eddie's thin neck.

"Hey, what're you doing?" Eddie tried to say. Nothing came out though, because Darrin was squeezing too hard. Eddie struggled uselessly. Even his good arm wasn't strong enough to make Darrin loosen his hold. A hard kick in the shins with his orthopedic shoe might have done it. Eddie wished he'd listened to the doctor and worn those way onto his feet with one outsized hand. "What happened to you?"

"Darrin got my money. I'm going to the office and report him." Eddie was so angry he sputtered which kept Gary from understanding him. Having to repeat himself to *Gary,* of all people, frustrated Eddie even more.

When he finally understood, Gary said, "Don't report him, Eddie. He'll get you for it if you do."

"So what can he do, slice my ears off?"

"Maybe. He's mean."

"But he stole Mina's birthday present—the money for the elf."

"Oh, yeah, Mina's birthday present. Gee," Gary said and stood there thinking. He was a big guy. He looked like a high school kid with his thick shoulders and the brown hairs of a mustache already showing on his upper lip, even though he was only a year older than Eddie, twelve to Eddie's eleven. But thinking wasn't what Gary did best.

"Tell you what," Gary said. "I'll borrow the elf from the store, and you pay for it when you can."

"You crazy? Your father'd send you to jail if he caught you."

"He won't catch me."

"You always say that and he does every time."

"Listen, he won't even notice. You think he knows half the stuff he's got in that store? He buys boxes that he don't even open up to see what kind of stuff's inside."

"Forget it. I'll get the money some other way."

The bell rang. They were the last kids outside the school. Gary held the door open and Eddie limped in. His throat was sore from Darrin's squeezing, but that wasn't what made him determined to complain to the principal; it was the money. He only had three days until Mina's birthday. In three days, he couldn't even get enough together for a coloring book, which was what he'd bought her last year and the year before. Rocking unevenly from bad leg to good, he thrust himself past the row of lockers outside their classroom.

"Eddie, where you going?" Gary asked.

"Office," Eddie said. He slung around the corner and aimed himself through the door of the principal's office before Gary could grab him back. A pack of glum-looking fourth graders was jammed onto the benches, and an irate bus driver was in the principal's office. Eddie could hear him yelling through the closed door about kids tripping each other in the aisles. The second bell rang. Late for homeroom. He had better remember to ask for a pass.

"I got a problem," he said to the secretary.

"What, Eddie?" She looked up from the rosters she was checking, her pencil poised over a name.

"I need to see Mr. B. I got mugged," Eddie said.

She frowned. "I'm sorry. What did you say?"

He took a deep breath and began again slowly. If he gave each word its due, people understood him better, but the phone rang. The secretary held up a finger to ask him to wait. Then the new aide came over wanting to know how to do something and looking anxious.

"You come back later when we're not so busy, Eddie," the secretary said as she answered the phone.

Discouraged, he asked for a pass. That she understood. She scribbled one for him with her free hand, and he left.

Gary, sitting in the back of the room where they always sat, raised his eyebrows questioningly. Eddie shook his head as he handed the pass to purse-mouthed Miss Clark who was writing their assignment on the board. Miss Clark looked at him with distaste. He'd seen back in September that she hadn't been too pleased to get a kid with special needs. All year he'd been trying to prove to her that he wasn't going to be any trouble, but she still wasn't convinced. Miss Clark was the kind of person who couldn't tolerate weeds, raggedy edges on paper, or anything noisy. He made it down the aisle to his seat next to Gary without knocking into anything and sat down.

"Did you see him?" Gary whispered.

"He was busy."

"You're lucky," Gary said. "They would have sliced your ears off for sure."

While Eddie did the section in the math workbook on pie charts, he was trying to think of how he could get Mina her elf without letting Gary steal it for him. He couldn't mow lawns or wash windows like his fifteen-year-old brother, Tom, who was in high school, or get a real job like his two oldest brothers. He couldn't even babysit for other kids, although he did it for Mina every day until Mom got home from work. But no other mother was going to trust a kid with cerebral palsy to babysit, even though Eddie knew he was good at the job. Mina said he was the best, and Mom claimed it relieved her mind considerably to know she had *him* to rely on while she did her dietitian's job at the hospital. Mom had offered to pay him, but Eddie had said, "No thanks." He was proud that he could pitch in like his brothers to help make her salary stretch. The last year while Dad was dying had put the family in debt, and Mom had it tough anyway, keeping a six-person family going by herself.

Eddie began imagining the scene in the principal's office when Darrin would be called in to answer to Eddie's accusation. "Me?" Darrin would say, the picture of innocence. "I didn't take his money. I wasn't even in the school this morning. We didn't have wrestling practice. Ask the coach."

Even supposing the principal believed Eddie, that didn't mean he'd get his money back. They could search Darrin, but probably he was too smart to be carrying it, and if he had it on him, so what. One five dollar bill looked just like another. Eddie wished he'd marked it. He should have marked it, carried it in his shoe, or better yet, not brought it to school at all.

"You haven't gotten very far with your workbook, Eddie." Miss Clark's voice pricked at his back. "Daydreaming, are you?"

"Ungh." Eddie swallowed.

"Well, you can stay in for recess and do it then," Miss Clark said, "you and Gary."

Gary looked up at her, sad eyed. He loved playing kickball during recess. The only time he liked school was when he was kicking the ball halfway across the field in a game. He would have gone out for football last fall if he hadn't had to work in his father's store, but his father said he needed Gary's help afternoons and Saturdays.

Gary had been struggling all period to fill in the pie chart with the right fractions. He'd erased his answers until he'd almost worn through the page. It wasn't not working that had kept him from finishing. It was not understanding.

"If we get the assignment done, can we go to recess?" Eddie asked Miss Clark.

She looked at him hard, unwilling to admit she hadn't understood.

"He wants to know if we get the assignment done, if we can—" Gary began translating.

"Certainly," Miss Clark snapped as if she'd understood all along, and she hastened back down the aisle to the safety of her desk.

Eddie switched workbooks with Gary. At the end of the math period, Gary's book had a completed assignment. Eddie had bad handwriting, but luckily, his number writing was neat enough to pass for Gary's.

"Thanks," Gary whispered when Eddie handed him back the workbook that was his ticket to recess. "You're a pal."

Eddie had about decided not to report Darrin but to get revenge on him some other way. What he hadn't figured out was how to get Mina's elf. Missing recess would allow him to sit in the empty classroom, pretending to labor over the pie chart, while he thought. He could enjoy the quiet and ignore Miss Clark who was marking papers with her lips pinned shut. He did mind, though, that the only solution that came to him was to ask his brothers to lend him money again.

It made him feel like such a baby to have to ask for a loan. Tom wouldn't have any extra cash. He spent everything he made on the car he and his friend were rebuilding against the time when they'd have drivers' licenses. Walter, who'd gone to work in a body shop after high school graduation, was the best one to borrow from because money didn't matter to him, and he didn't mind lending what he had. As an accountant, Martin earned the most, but Martin lent money grudgingly even when it was Mom who needed to hit him up for a loan. Walter was the one to ask first.

The anger soured in Eddie's gut. He'd give anything to be able to hammer the money out of Darrin. Nothing would make him feel better than getting back at that kid.

The five dollars Darrin had stolen should have been in Gary's pocket. The plan had been that Gary'd wait until his father was out of the store, then he'd pocket the elf and stick the money for it in the cash register. The junky little green-and-yellow ceramic man had to be priced at less than five dollars, but if Mr. Winowski knew Eddie was the buyer, he was likely to jack up the cost. Gary's father hated Eddie. He'd hated him from the first day Gary had brought Eddie to the store.

That day had started out as the most exciting in Eddie's life. He'd transferred to a third grade class in a regular school after spending years going to school in the Center for the Disabled. He was finally getting a chance to be a regular kid. Despite the weak muscles on his left side, he could walk without a brace—sometimes; and he could write and talk—sort of. Besides, his teachers in the Center claimed he was able enough mentally to make up for what he couldn't do physically.

Right away he'd matched up with Gary, grin for

grin, and after school, Gary had taken him into The Treasure Shop to meet his father. Only as he was leaving for home, Eddie had heard Mr. Winowski ask his son, "Is a cripple the best you can do for a friend?"

"He's a good kid," Gary had said.

"Yeah? Good enough for *you* maybe," Mr. Winowski had sneered.

Having his best friend's father hate him had bothered Eddie until he'd finally realized Mr. Winowski didn't appear to like anybody much, not even his customers, and least of all Gary.

Mina's birthday. Eddie brought his mind back to the problem. How was he going to get the money to buy her that elf now?

2

Enter the Dragon

He didn't plan to tell them about getting mugged. Brothers or mother, one or the other would insist on rushing off to school to fight for him. Their attempts to protect him always made Eddie feel like a baby, or else the way Mr. Winowski saw him, as "the cripple."

Eddie waited until his brothers were flipping TV channels in the living room and Mina had gone to bed to ask, "Anybody got an extra five bucks I could borrow?"

"What'd you do with the five you got as a reward from that woman in the parking lot, spend it already?" Martin asked. He wasn't an accountant by accident.

"I didn't spend it. It got lost."

"Where'd you lose it?"

Eddie squirmed. He never lied to his family. "In school."

"Well, did you report the loss to the office?"

"Hey, Martin," Walter said, rotating the metal weight he was using to strengthen his wrists from one hand to the other, "lend the kid the five, and I'll pay you back when I get my paycheck. Okay?"

"I'm just finding out what's going on," Martin said. "Anything wrong with that?"

"Did you have trouble in school again, Eddie?" Mom asked. He'd thought she was totally absorbed in letting out the seams on her new green uniform to accommodate what she called her "derrière," her ample rear end. Her eyes remained on her work, but apparently her ears were tuned to her sons' conversation.

"Ah, jeez!" Eddie gave up. "Darrin got me. Darrin gets everybody, not just me."

"So what did the principal do about it?" Martin asked.

"I didn't tell him. I was going to, but I didn't."

"Smart move," Tom put in. He was lying on his stomach reading *A Separate Peace* for English, mostly during the TV commercials. "The best way to handle that punk is we stand him on his ear and warn him off Eddie," Tom advised his two older brothers. Tom considered himself the practical one in the family. Once Eddie had heard him tagging them all to his buddy as they fixed Tom's bike. Mom was good natured; Martin was boring; Walter was physical; Tom was practical; Eddie was sharp; and Mina was a pint-sized character.

"I'm not beating up on eleven-year-olds," Walter said. He was brawny from working out at the Y after his job at the body shop.

"I'll speak to the principal," Mom said. "That Darrin's a menace. Somebody's got to control him."

"Mom, please," Eddie begged. "Let me handle it myself."

They all looked at him, their faces marked with disbelief, doubt, concern. "You can't, Eddie," Tom said. "He could snap you like a toothpick."

"Well, I wasn't gonna punch him out," Eddie drawled. The way he said it made them laugh, and they let the matter drop.

After Eddie finished brushing his teeth that night, he found the five dollars on his pillow. No way to tell who'd put it there, but he'd pay it back to whoever had.

Darrin had a wrestling match that Thursday. He strutted down the hall so full of himself that he looked right through Eddie as they passed each other. Later Eddie heard that Darrin had won.

"I'll get him back. You'll see," Eddie assured Gary and handed over the borrowed five dollars for the elf. Gary was going to be in the store alone that afternoon. Buying the elf would be a cinch for him.

* * *

Mina beamed when she saw Eddie waiting for her outside her kindergarten classroom Thursday afternoon. She ran to put herself into his hands as trustingly as if he were any regular big brother. It gave him a charge, the way she was unaware of his bum arm and leg and never noticed his difficulty getting his tongue around words. Tom wasn't so bad that way either. Martin and Walter were the ones who'd boost Eddie up high steps without asking, or hold doors open for him, or carry packages he could manage by himself.

"Are we going to the park?" Mina asked, while Eddie was showing the driver the special passes that allowed them to get off in town instead of at their home stop.

"First we pick up Gary," Eddie said. "He left for the store after recess." Gary's father had to go to an auction and hadn't been willing to close the store for the afternoon. It wasn't legal to leave a child in charge, but Mr. Winowski had told Gary to lie about his age if anyone asked questions.

Eddie heaved himself up the stairs with his good arm and leg, dragging the rest of him after.

"I hope the ducks are hungry. I saved half my sandwich for them," Mina said. Fiercely, she added, "Don't you let Gary scare them this time."

"He was just fooling around trying to be funny last week, Mina."

"I know *that*, but the ducks didn't," Mina said.

Eddie laughed. Mina tickled him; she was such

a sharp little peanut. "Well, don't worry. If he scares the ducks, I'll beat him up." He meant to be funny, but Mina didn't laugh at the idea of her skinny brother beating up big, beefy Gary. No doubt she thought he could.

They sat side by side in the first seat and got off at the foot of Meat Market Hill. It was back of the main street in town. On one side of Meat Market Hill was a bar with a beer sign filling its window; on the other was a vacuum cleaner repair shop. The few private houses had garbage pails lined up in front of them instead of lawns. The Treasure Shop was in the fifth building on the right.

Knowing Gary's father wouldn't be there, Eddie walked in boldly, past the glass case with the old jewelry, past shelves and tables of battered electric coffee pots and music boxes and eyeglass cases and knickknacks. Gary was in the back, which was jammed with used furniture, sitting in a rocking chair looking at a comic book.

"You're not going to like what I got to tell you," Gary said, the instant he spotted Eddie.

"You gave somebody the wrong change again?"

"Worse than that." Gary looked serious. Without his usual goofy grin, he was a good-looking boy, or he would be if he didn't hunch over as if he were apologizing for his size.

"Tell me," Eddie said.

"I sold the elf."

"You *what*?" Eddie looked around quickly, but

Mina hadn't followed him into the store. She was still standing outside studying the showcase where the best items were set out to catch a passerby's interest. "What'd you do that for?"

"This old lady come in and asked to see it," Gary said. "I told her it was sold, and she goes, 'Well, why's it in the window then? And where's your father, young man?' Then she asks how come I'm not in school. She had me so shook I handed the elf over without thinking. And guess what, the price on the bottom was only three bucks. She made me give her a receipt. 'I know your father,' she goes, like she's going to turn me in. I'm sorry, Eddie, but she rattled me."

"Okay, okay. It was just a piece of junk," Eddie said to make Gary feel better. "Mina's probably found something else she likes."

Immediately, they went outside to check the theory out.

"My elf's gone," Mina said. "Did you bring him inside, Gary?"

"No," Gary said. "Someone bought it. I'm sorry, Mina."

"Oh," Mina said. "Me too." She heaved a sigh. Then she pointed. "That dragon's staring at me."

"What?" Eddie followed her finger to a slinky brass dragon with six-inch blue glass wings edged in lead. Its glittering red eyes seemed alive. Eddie blinked. Had the snaky body wriggled just now, or was the afternoon sunlight playing tricks?

"You like that dragon?" Gary asked Mina eagerly. "Pop just hung it in the window today. He got it from a mystery box, you know, a box he bought that he didn't know what was inside it? Sometimes he gets good stuff that way, but mostly it's throw-away garbage."

"I don't know if he likes me," Mina said about the dragon.

"Sure he likes you, Mina," Gary said. "Everybody likes you."

"Umm," Mina said. "Are we going to feed the ducks now?"

"I got to wait for my old man to get back," Gary said.

"You see something else you like, Mina?" Eddie asked hopefully.

"I'd like to feed the ducks," Mina said, and her small, expressive face locked up tight.

"Okay, okay. We'll go." Eddie exchanged looks with Gary who knew how stubborn Mina could be. She wasn't about to admit to liking anything but the elf in this mood. "Come when you can, Gare."

The park was a disappointment. The ducks weren't really hungry. Too many young mothers with toddlers had probably already fed them. As to Gary, he didn't make it that afternoon which didn't surprise Eddie much. Mr. Winowski was often later than he said he'd be.

* * *

Eddie sat brooding in the kitchen after supper. Since the supermarket was the only store he could walk to from home, he'd have to buy Mina's present there. She wasn't much for fish or fruit. So his choices were limited to candy or a coloring book, or maybe candy *and* a coloring book if he didn't get new crayons, boring gifts for a kid sister as special as Mina.

Mom was working on her checkbook at the other end of the kitchen table. Eddie leaned over and asked, "What's something good I could get Mina for her birthday, Mom?"

"A coloring book's always nice," she murmured absently.

Just then the doorbell rang.

"Hey," Gary said when Eddie let him in. "You ready to do the social studies assignment?"

Eddie had forgotten all about it, but he led Gary upstairs right away. A week ago, when the social studies teacher had tried to give Gary an oral quiz on his work, he had folded his long arms and answered, "I dunno," to everything she had asked him.

"Do you *want* to fail social studies and end up repeating sixth grade?" Mrs. Halstead had asked Gary worriedly.

"That's okay," Gary had told her. "I got to go to school 'til I'm sixteen anyway. What's the difference what grade I'm in when I get done?" He'd sounded as if he really didn't care, Eddie had thought as he sat listening next to Gary. Sometimes Gary could be as stubborn as Mina.

"But how are you going to get a job?" Mrs. Halstead had pleaded.

"I already know how to work the cash register, and I'm good with customers. I can be a storekeeper like my father," Gary said.

"And that's all you think you need to know about life?"

"I know a lot about life, just not much about social studies, Mrs. Halstead." Gary had grinned amiably at the soft, gray-faced teacher. Mrs. Halstead always looked tired, but at least she didn't yell much.

"Maybe if I worked with Gary," Eddie offered.

Mrs. Halstead had frowned at Eddie, and he'd begun patiently repeating what he'd said, thinking she hadn't understood him, but she stopped him. "I heard you," she said. "That's not a bad idea. If you researched the answers and Gary wrote them down, I'd get good work out of both of you."

Eddie had been embarrassed. He knew his handwriting was bad, and he couldn't blame it on c.p. either, because he wrote with his right hand, which wasn't on his affected side. Gary, big as he was, wrote small and neatly.

Upstairs in Eddie's room, Gary bumped his head against the low ceiling above the table Eddie used as a desk. Gary always bumped his head when they worked at that table. "I got something for you," he said as he sat down, stretching his long legs out. Eddie opened the notebook he'd pulled off the pile on the table and looked up. There was the brass dragon with its blue wings, dangling from a fishline a foot from his nose.

"How'd you get that out of the store?"

"I took it while I was waiting for my father. I figured you could give it to Mina. Remember, she thought it was live?"

The dragon looked beautiful to Eddie. Its bright blue glass wings were shaped like a butterfly's. The snaky curves of its polished brass body were marked with scales, and its red glass eyes sparked. "This has to cost more than five bucks," he said.

"Nah. Anyway, you don't have to pay for it. He may not even notice it's gone. You take it, Eddie. Mina might like it more than the elf. I feel bad that I sold her elf."

Eddie considered. Then he offered, "I'll take the dragon if you take the money. You can say you forgot to put it in the cash register or something if he's already noticed the dragon's gone."

"Then he'll be *sure* I did something bad."

"Well, all right. We'll think of something else. But I've got to pay for Mina's present." Finally Gary accepted the five dollar bill Eddie had safely stowed inside the paper cover of his social studies book.

It was ten o'clock before Gary left for home. He

liked hanging around Eddie's house because Mom was always willing to chat during commercials. Eddie's brothers blew in and out, and Mina sat in the middle of the living room, totally absorbed in make believe games with her dolls or in drawing pictures. "No way you could ever get lonesome in this place," Gary often said.

Once he'd told Eddie, "I used to feel sorry for you because, you know, you've got cerebral palsy, but forget that. You're a lucky kid, Eddie."

Eddie knew what his friend meant. He'd been to Gary's house and seen the grungy kitchen where Eddie and his father hung out, eating, watching TV, reading the newspapers that littered surfaces not covered with pots or dishes or paper bags. The Winowskis' living room was worse, a ghostly place, hung with spider webs and layered with dust. And Gary's bedroom was a fortress built of comic books. Popular music played on his tape deck whether he was in the room or not.

Gary said the house had been nice when his mother was alive, but after she died, The Treasure Shop became all his father cared about.

Getting ready for bed that night, Eddie draped a tee shirt over the dragon on the night table by his bed. In the morning, he'd wrap the dragon for Mina's birthday.

He lay in bed tackling the other problem in his life. Darrin. Letting a kid like Darrin get away with anything was asking for more of the same.

Probably it would have been smart to return and speak to the principal. Better that than have his older brothers go shake Darrin up. Best of all would be to do something himself. What though?

An image of the kid in the electric wheelchair at the Center For The Disabled came into his mind. The kid had gotten mad at a big, bearded, physical therapist who insisted they had to work through the pain. That big healthy guy hadn't looked like he knew what pain was. One afternoon the kid had aimed his wheelchair right at the therapist and knocked him over on his butt. Eddie had been thrilled. What a show of power from a kid who sat strapped into a foam cushioned chair with just enough strength to press the control buttons!

How great it would be if just once he could be strong enough to knock Darrin down. Just once would give him satisfaction enough to last a lifetime.

Eddie closed his eyes, glad nobody could see into his mind. He knew it was wrong to want to beat people up, even if they deserved it. Mom would be disgusted, but Mina—Mina would understand. She had the family temper, she and Tom and Eddie. Mom said they'd inherited it from their father.

Eddie yawned. He'd forgotten to practice his phrasing, speaking into the tape recorder that the speech pathologist had lent him. He was supposed to read the passages she'd marked for him into the recorder and listen to hear how he sounded. People would understand him if he got his breath and tongue coordinated better, she said. Of course, the people he cared about already understood him okay, but if he wanted to become a psychologist, he'd have to improve. Sleepily, he closed his eyes. Tomorrow. Tomorrow, he'd do it.

That night Eddie had a dream. He knew it was a dream because nothing like it could happen in reality. The tee shirt on the table beside his pillow began to heave as if something live were under it trying to get out. Eddie sat bolt upright in bed and stared. The tee shirt was not only heaving, but making snorting, hissing noises. Eddie was too scared to breathe.

Suddenly, the tee shirt slipped off the table. There was the dragon, blue wings now big as a hawk's, bigger. They filled the air above the bed, and the brass body writhed in snaky, sinewy curves. But most awesome of all were the eyes, like red embers, aimed at Eddie. He gagged on his fear and pulled the cover over his head. Shaking, he waited for some hideous, horrible thing to happen to him.

A warm weight touched his shoulder. Eddie choked and lay still.

The weight remained peacefully against him. He snuck the cover down from his eyes so that he could peer over it. Wings folded, the dragon lay snuggled against his side. Its snaky head rested trustingly right below Eddie's cheek.

For a long moment, Eddie lay marveling at the strangeness of his dream. Then a purring began against his throat for all the world as if the dragon were a contented cat. Nice, Eddie thought, so long as he didn't end up being bitten next.

"You comfortable?" Eddie asked the dragon in his dream. He didn't expect an answer. Even dreaming, he wasn't crazy enough to imagine dragons talked. With his good right hand, he dared himself to touch its hide. It felt warm, satiny, and now in the half light from the street lamps outside his window, he could see that the wings weren't stiff anymore but some rustling material, as flexible and strong as a plastic kite.

"Now what?" Eddie asked himself. He'd always wanted a pet. Was he getting a dragon instead of a dog? Weird. And weirder yet was thinking it was weird to be having a weird dream while he was having one.

In the morning he woke up to find the dragon back in its brass and glass form under the tee shirt. As far as Eddie could tell, the dream had been just that. He wished he could tell Mina about it, but he couldn't until after he'd given her the dragon, and maybe not then because it might scare her.

Today felt like one of his tired days; so he put his molded plastic brace on, closed the velcro straps and covered the contraption with his jeans. Again he rejected the orthopedic shoes. The tee shirt which had hidden the dragon was clean. He pulled it on, bad arm first, then good. He was stowing the dragon in his closet to keep Mina from seeing it too soon, when he noticed the white sticker near its tail for the first time. Five dollars Gary had said, but the price on the sticker was clearly fifteen. Trust Gary to miss the one in front of the five.

Fifteen dollars! Mr. Winowski would kill Gary for taking five for it, never mind whether or not he'd remembered to put the money in the cash register. The dragon had to go back in the store. Gary's hide was more important than giving Mina a special present. She was going to end up with a coloring book again after all. Maybe there'd be one with Snow White in the supermarket. Mina loved Snow White.

3

Who Pays?

Eddie wrapped the dragon in a torn tee shirt from his mother's rag box to protect its wings, tucked it into his backpack with his lunch and math book, and set off for school.

"You missed a one on the price tag, Gare," Eddie said. He slung his backpack onto his desk and dropped into his seat next to Gary in the back of the room. "That dragon costs fifteen bucks."

"I know," Gary said. "Here's your five back."

Eddie dug out the lumpy tee shirt package and tried to put it on Gary's desk, but Gary pushed it away. "Keep it," he said. "I told my father someone stole it."

"Why'd you do that?"

"'Cause he was giving me a hard time about where his fifteen dollar dragon was, and when I heard fifteen dollars, it blew my mind. I just gave him this story about a girl asking to look at it and how it was gone after she left the store."

"So what'd he do to you?"

"Yelled. And he's making me pay it off by working for nothing, but so what? He always finds *some* excuse not to pay me."

"Yeah, but if I don't pay, I'll feel like *I* stole it," Eddie said. "Tell you what. You can say the girl felt so guilty she brought the dragon back. How's that?"

Gary shook his head stubbornly. "You keep it, Eddie."

"I can't. Unless I pay for it."

"How? You only got five bucks."

"I can get the other ten eventually."

"What are you going to do? Not eat lunch for a year? You're already too skinny to keep your pants up."

"Deposit bottles!" Eddie said. The inspiration popped him upright in his seat. "Remember last summer?" They had found enough bottles in the woods to buy themselves ice cream sundaes one steamy, green July afternoon. "I bet we'd find a fortune in bottles there now."

Gary cheered up. "Yeah, maybe. I'd meet you after school, but I gotta work. How about Sunday? You bring Mina's red wagon like last time, and I'll bring garbage bags."

Miss Clark called homeroom to order then, and

they had to be quiet. Immediately the drawbacks to their plan came into Eddie's mind. The woods were dangerous. Kids went there to do drugs, drink and smoke. A child's body had been found last year, and the police still hadn't caught the murderer. Also, the rumor was Darrin's gang had a shack up there.

Eddie hoisted himself to his feet for the pledge of allegiance. What are you going to do, he asked himself impatiently, go through life scared to take a risk? The woods were okay most of the time. He'd go and not worry.

Eddie was standing on a chair outside the social studies room taking down class reports from the unit before the one they'd just finished. Another of Mrs. Halstead's good qualities was she never questioned his ability to do a job. If he offered, she let him. He was leaning against the wall for balance, trying to get the topmost report which was just out of reach, when Anita Valdez came down the hall. Anita was tall and beautiful with quiet hazel eyes and shiny brown hair that bounced on her shoulders. Eddie had had a crush on her since third grade.

"Want me to get that for you, Eddie?" she asked.

"Thanks," he said. "If I grew a couple of more inches, I could reach, but Mrs. Halstead probably can't wait that long."

Anita's smile was radiant. It made Eddie so giddy he nearly fell off the chair. When he'd gotten himself down, almost stepping on the backpack on the floor beside the chair, she climbed on and handed the report to him.

Footsteps pounded along the empty hallway. Darrin in a hurry to get somewhere. "Stop looking up her skirt, Eddie." Darrin tossed the command out like a dirty snowball as he ran past.

The report slipped through Eddie's fingers. He crouched awkwardly to pick it up, which put him in an even worse position relative to the skirt. Flushing, he said, "I wasn't."

Anita gave him an odd look. Eddie shriveled as if he were really guilty.

"It's okay," she said. "Darrin's just a loud mouth." She jumped off the chair, said she better get going, and took off down the hall without giving Eddie time to thank her, or say she'd made his day. He'd meant to say that, like a compliment. Darrin ruined everything. It had taken three years for Anita to pay any attention to Eddie, and he hadn't even managed to say something nice to her. "I wish he'd drop dead," Eddie muttered.

He shoved the chair back into the empty social studies room and laid the old reports on Mrs. Halstead's desk. Then he returned to the hall to retrieve his backpack and get on to gym class. What he saw stopped him short.

The dragon was surging out of the backpack, inflating like a long balloon as it came. No sooner was it out, than its snaky body skidded down the tiled floor, and the blue wings flapped open, filling half the hallway. It flew past rows of lockers and the closed classroom doors, turning the same corner Darrin had turned. Eddie had time to blink in amazement and doubt what he'd seen before he heard someone yell.

"Yeow!" A bang, then footsteps running. By the time Eddie reached the corner, all he saw were more lockers, bulletin boards, and the deserted hallway.

He shook his head to wake himself out of his daydream and returned to get his backpack which was still outside Mrs. Halstead's door. Just in case, he opened the pack and prodded the rag-wrapped dragon in the bottom. Naturally it was still there. He'd always known he had a pretty good imagination, but now he wondered if maybe it wasn't too good.

Then on the sidewalk outside the school while waiting for the bus, he heard something that gave him the shivers. "Did you hear Darrin broke his finger? Yeah, he jammed it against the gym door," Richard was saying to Mack. Eddie stumbled, almost falling in his shock. The glass and metal dragon in the pack dug into his back. Just glass and metal. It couldn't have had anything to do with Darrin breaking a finger. Could it? But if the yell of pain Eddie had heard after the dragon turned the corner was Darrin—some coincidence that was. Some dragon!

Mina's birthday party on Saturday was a little disappointing. She'd invited only one friend. Mom had tried to persuade her to invite more, but Mina had said, "I just like Sara. All I want is her, and you and my brothers, Mommy."

But Sara couldn't come because she was sick. Mina didn't seem to mind too much. She blew out her birthday candles and clapped for herself, then began excitedly unwrapping her presents, except for the tricycle Martin and Walter had gotten her. It was pink with streamers on the handles, and they hadn't wrapped it. Tom had bought her a doll. Mom gave her clothes, and Eddie gave her the dragon, wrapped in red tissue paper from Christmas, placed inside a shoe box tied with a red ribbon.

When Mina saw the dragon, she said, "Oh." Without looking at Eddie or taking the dragon out of the box, she thanked him for it politely.

The rest of the family seemed impressed with Eddie's gift. They exclaimed over it and complimented him on picking such an unusual present. Their fuss distracted him from examining Mina's reaction. Later she carried all her presents, except for the tricycle, up to her bedroom. Then she and Mom and Eddie went to see a cartoon movie about a cat. The movie was supposed to be funny, but

Mina watched it with unsmiling intensity. Eddie suspected she took all the disasters the cat kept getting into too much to heart.

One of the villains in the movie had a smile that reminded Eddie of Darrin. Like Darrin, the movie villain seemed to enjoy hurting people. Eddie wondered if meanness was something you were born with, like cerebral palsy. He didn't think Darrin could have learned it from his parents, the joke-happy dentist who took care of Eddie's teeth and the gentle, earnest dental technician who was his wife. If anybody was going to learn meanness, it ought to be Gary, but nasty as his father was, Gary was a good guy. It must be people were born mean.

Miss Clark was the only other mean person Eddie knew personally. Well, maybe she wasn't mean, just crabby. Probably her problem was that she didn't like teaching. Or it could be she was afraid of people with disabilities. Eddie had seen visitors look scared when they came into the Center for the Disabled. They'd sneak looks at kids in wheelchairs and braces, with droopy heads and spastic limbs and hands and feet that turned backwards, and draw away if any got too close.

"I guess they think it's catching," Eddie had once joked with Mrs. Leibowitz, who was the Center's psychologist and his favorite person there.

"I think you're right, Eddie," Mrs. Leibowitz had agreed.

She was the one who'd convinced Eddie he was smart. "You're a very perceptive boy," she'd assured him often. "You understand people better than most adults." Thanks to Mrs. Leibowitz, he'd finally begun feeling good about himself. No wonder he'd liked her best.

"So did you like the movie?" Eddie asked Mina on the way home.

"It was okay."

"Well, *I* enjoyed it very much," Mom said, straight-faced. Eddie got a laugh out of that. Mom had slept through the whole movie.

He was reading a science fiction story in bed that night about a planet where everybody had to live underground because there wasn't any atmosphere. All of a sudden Mina appeared two inches from his nose, making him jump.

"Eddie?"

"What? What's the matter?"

"He's watching me."

"Who? Who, Mina?"

"The dragon. Don't be mad, but I don't want him." She thrust the shoe box with the dragon in it at Eddie.

"You don't want the dragon?"

"No. He scares me." She leaned over and whispered in Eddie's ear, "I think he's alive."

A chill ran down Eddie's back. He wanted to ask her what made her say that, but she scooted out of his room, leaving him with the shoe box. He took the dragon out and studied it. Brass and glass. Nothing that solid and cold could transform itself into a live dragon, even if such things as dragons existed. "Crazy," he told himself. "You read too much science fiction." He set the dragon on the night table again.

Briefly, he considered returning it to Gary and discovered that he didn't want to. Not that the dragon was magic. Eddie didn't really believe that. But it was handsome, and it did have something special about it, a kind of feeling, or maybe the feeling was in him. He'd sleep on it, he decided, and make up his mind in the morning.

Before he was quite awake the next morning, Eddie had the dream again, the one where the dragon stretched its head out and purred against Eddie's shoulder like a pet.

He woke up feeling good. Maybe they could collect enough bottles to make up the fifteen dollars. Twenty now. He'd have to buy Mina something else for her birthday. Twenty dollars worth of bottles was an awful lot of red wagons full, a whole mess of garbage bags full. But it was the only way he could think of to make money. Five dollars to repay the anonymous family donor and fifteen to clear his conscience with Mr. Winowski, and so that Gary wouldn't stay a liar and a thief. That was a big debt for an eleven year old kid. Well, he'd work on it.

4

Collecting Deposit Bottles and Cans

On the far side of the hill, a four lane interstate highway cut off the woods. A culvert, strewn with junked cars and box springs, made the near side of the hill difficult to reach except by a single footpath. The town maintained a city park—the one Eddie took Mina to for its duck pond and playground—but only the woods offered privacy and adventure as well.

The hill was so steep Eddie had a hard time climbing it. Even though he was pulling the wagon, Gary reached the bald spot on top, where kids did their partying and built illegal camp fires, long before Eddie. He arrived to find the red wagon abandoned in the middle of the clearing and no friend in sight. A chuckle gave Gary away. He was perched like an oversized eagle in the thick-leaved branches of the climbing tree. Its lower branches had broken off in stubs, providing a natural ladder.

"So how far can you see from up there?" Eddie asked.

"To downtown. I can see the bank building and the clock on the courthouse."

"Yeah?" Eddie was envious. Briefly, he considered trying to climb up too, but it would be hard, and maybe impossible, with only one good leg and arm. Besides, he'd use up all the energy he was going to need for collecting.

He spied a litter of beer cans near the flat rocks and set to work. By the time Gary dropped from the tree, Eddie had picked up all the deposit cans and bottles in sight, half a garbage bag full.

"Looks like nobody's been collecting here for a while," Eddie said with satisfaction. "Wish we had a rake for the ones under the leaves. You want to find me a good stick to rake with?"

Agreeably, Gary went stick hunting in the woods while Eddie explored the edges of the bald area. "Here," Gary said, handing Eddie a strong forked stick.

"You going to help pick up?"

"Nah, you got what's here. I'll climb back up in the tree and be the lookout."

"Lookout for what?"

"The enemy."

"We don't need a lookout. We need a worker."

grow up," Eddie said fiercely. "I don't care how hard it is, just so I keep getting there."

Gary sighed and said, "You make me tired."

"Why?"

"Listening to you. It makes me tired to think about all you got to do."

"Well, and you? Don't you want to be somebody?"

"I want to be a pro football player."

"So?"

"So how am I going to play football if my father never lets me out of the store for practice?"

"You could make him let you out. If you want to play bad enough, you could find a way to make him."

Silence from up in the tree. Eddie decided he'd rested long enough and went foraging along a faint trail through the underbrush looking for an undiscovered deposit bottle gold mine. He ran into a dead end shortly and came limping back to find Gary tossing cans at a rock.

"Hey, stop that, Gare. They won't pay me for wrecked cans."

"I said you didn't have to pay for the dragon. How come you gotta do that the hard way too?"

"Because that's how I am."

"Well you're stupid then."

"Okay, I'm stupid."

"Hey, I didn't mean that," Gary said. "I know you're smart, smarter than me anyways."

"Come on. Let's go to my house. We found all we're going to find here today."

"Looks like somebody's building back there in the woods." Gary nodded his head in the direction. "I saw it from the tree."

"Let's take a look," Eddie said.

"Okay. It might just be a pile of boards though."

They left the bag of deposits in the red wagon and set off. Gary broke trail for Eddie who realized his friend was still moody when Gary suddenly asked him, "What are you going to do about girls, Eddie? I mean when you're old enough to—you know."

Instantly, Eddie thought about Anita Valdez. He sighed deeply. Then he said, "I'll worry about it when I'm old enough."

"But I'm beginning to feel old enough now," Gary said.

Looking at Gary's already sprouted body, Eddie didn't doubt it. Even Darrin didn't have a mustache like Gary's. "So," Eddie said, "that's okay."

"But what girl's going to like a goofball like me?"

"They'll like you a lot better than me, Gare. Anyway, you'll be okay when you grow up."

"You think so?"

"Sure."

"I hope you're right," Gary said. He looked back at Eddie and grinned. "Anyway, here it is."

In front of them was a shack, set into the earth so that only the roof and the top of a wall protruded. The entrance was through the roof. Pine branches had been scattered over it as camouflage.

Gary pulled aside the plywood board that served as a door and leaned over the opening. "Dark down there," he said. "They got a table and some chairs. Oh, oh."

"Oh, oh, what?" Eddie asked from the ground outside.

"There's a knife sticking in the table."

"So, can we get in?"

"I don't know. I don't think we better fool around here, Eddie."

"See any deposits?"

Gary hesitated. Then he admitted, "Yeah, there's a pile in the corner."

"You want to lower me in so I can get them?"

"Okay, if you want."

Eddie gave Gary his good arm, and Gary hoisted him the three feet up onto the roof, then lowered him, gripping his good arm, into the dug out chamber in the earth below them. It looked as if the shack might have been built where a cave had been. Inside, it smelled of smoke and mold. After a minute, Eddie's eyes adjusted to the dimness, and he saw the rubbish pile full of deposit cans. He took off his shirt and made a pouch to hold them all. Gary reached down and took the filled pouch.

Then Eddie checked out the knife sticking in the table. Around it was a circle of names. Darrin's was all Eddie needed to see. "Let's get out of here, Gary," he said. "This is Darrin's place."

Gary reached down and clasped his good hand, but pulling Eddie up required more strength than lowering him had. "I can't do it," Gary grunted.

"Okay, let me think." Eddie's heart was racing. He couldn't imagine a worse place to get stuck. There. If he put a chair on top of the table— He spotted the ladder lying along the wall sideways then. That's how they did it, of course. It took all of Eddie's strength and more to work the ladder onto the table and lever it up so that Gary could reach it. Gary propped it against the side of the hole with its feet on the table. Eddie climbed the first rung.

"This is as far as I can get, Gare."

"Hang on," Gary told him and began pulling the ladder up with Eddie hanging on to it. By the time Gary had hauled him out of the hole, Eddie needed to lie on the cold, damp ground to regain some strength.

"You okay?" Gary asked when they'd rested.

"Yeah, I'm fine. Thanks."

"I think it's going to rain," Gary said.

"Yeah, let's get going."

They got back to the clearing and, without a word, Gary dumped the deposit cans into the bag,

help anybody stuck with a disability or a disease. Some things you needed help with no matter how hard you were willing to try.

Passing the parking lot on his way home, Eddie found a quarter. That lucky sign made him decide it had been a pretty good day after all.

Also, Gary's mood had changed thanks to the dragon. "Don't forget to bring it to school," was the last thing he'd said before heading home. He was excited about testing it. Actually, Eddie admitted to himself, he was excited about it too.

5

Siccing the Dragon

Gary was waiting for him. No sooner had Eddie finished maneuvering himself down the high step of the school bus than Gary asked, "Did you bring it?"

"Yeah. It's in my backpack." Eddie felt silly. There he stood, smack in the middle of the real world. Bright yellow and purple crocuses bobbed around the flagpole from which the stars and stripes flapped boldly in the wind. It had rained during the night, and puddles gleamed in the cheerful April sunlight. It was all there to see, nothing hidden, nothing magic, certainly not a dragon that did in the enemy.

"So who are we going to sic it on first?" Gary rubbed his hands together grinning.

"Cool it, Gare. I don't know how to *make* it do anything."

"Okay, but if it decides to take off, you better tell me."

"Uh," Eddie said. He didn't know if he was more disgusted with himself for having the fantasy or with Gary for believing in it.

By mid-morning, Eddie was so involved with school routines that he'd forgotten the dragon in the shoe box at the bottom of his backpack. Mrs. Halstead was talking about the Revolutionary War and why some people were loyal to England and why some had decided to revolt. He knew most of what she was saying because he'd been reading a history series called *WE WERE THERE*. Ms. Krantz, the librarian, had turned him onto it.

"Does anybody know what the Boston Tea Party was about?" Mrs. Halstead asked.

Eddie raised his hand. He'd just read a rousing description of how the patriots in Boston had dressed up as Indians and dumped English tea into Boston's harbor to protest the high English tax on it. "Eddie?" Mrs. Halstead smiled at him.

He started right at the beginning, telling page by page what the book had said, down to how the patriots had dyed their skins and gotten their feathers. It delighted him to be sharing what he'd learned, and his enthusiasm grew as he got to the most exciting part, how they snuck onto the ship at night.

Suddenly, Mrs. Halstead interrupted him. "Thank you, Eddie. Thank you. That was an impressive contribution."

He waited with his mouth open ready to finish, but she began hurriedly summarizing what he'd just told the class, as if—as if they might not have understood him. He turned cold. Had *she* understood him? Had anyone? The pounding in his ears kept him from hearing anything else until class was over.

Anita Valdez had stayed behind to talk to Mrs. Halstead. Eddie waited for Anita in the hall. If Gary had been present, he would have told Eddie the truth, but Gary had gone to the bathroom and hadn't come back. He did that sometimes when he got bored in class.

"Anita," Eddie said as she stepped into the hall. "You know when I was telling about the Boston Tea Party? Did you understand me?"

She hesitated. Then she said softly, "Not that well. You went so fast, Eddie."

"Yeah," he said. "Did you catch any of it?"

"Some." She shrugged, but it was the pity in her eyes that did him in altogether. Feeling sick, he let her walk away without another word.

Gary appeared behind him. "So, ready for lunch, Eddie-o?"

"Yeah."

They headed for the cafeteria in companionable silence. Gary took a tray. "You getting the tuna fish?"

Eddie always bought or brought something that didn't need to be chewed much, like tuna fish or egg salad. His tongue got in the way when he chewed, and he knew he looked gross unless he kept his mouth closed. "I don't feel much like eating today," Eddie answered Gary.

"Not even milk? You still saving to pay for the dragon?"

"All right, I'll get milk."

Two seats were left at the table where Anita was sitting with her friends. "Hey," Gary said. "You can sit by your girlfriend."

"No. I don't want to."

"How come? I thought you liked her." Gary looked puzzled.

Eddie shook his head stubbornly. Anita's pitying look was stuck in his mind. He stopped at a table piled high with art work, some class's posters. He and Gary could just squeeze in at the end.

"So if she did something to you, get the dragon to goose her," Gary joked.

"She didn't do anything." Eddie remembered what Gary had said in the woods on Sunday about his not talking clearly. Had he been overestimating his ability to communicate? It was true that to get through college, he needed to make himself understood. He'd better stop neglecting the exercises the speech pathologist had given him to do.

"You okay?" Gary asked with concern.

"Yeah, I'm fine."

"Looks like the gym teacher's out again; so we get to play softball outside." Eagerly Gary looked out the cafeteria window at the sun bright ballfield.

"If the sub lets us."

"She will, Eddie. She will."

She did too.

The hardest place for Eddie to forget that he was handicapped was the ballfield. No matter how often he told himself not to feel bad, that naturally they weren't going to pick a kid who couldn't run, it hurt when he was picked last or not at all. Today the team captains were Chris, who was a good kid, and a long-legged girl, a friend of Anita's. Darrin had told the sub he wanted to be team captain, but he must have done something that irritated her, because she wasn't letting him badger her into it.

"Shut up now or get off the field," she told him bluntly.

Darrin shut up and sulked until Chris picked him first. That cheered him up some.

It was tricky to set your face right, Eddie thought. He started by pretending to be watching the flag flap, as if he wasn't even interested in softball. Then he realized they might think he didn't want to be picked. Turning around, he stared hopefully right at the team captains.

Chris had just picked Gary. Usually Gary would urge whoever picked him to give Eddie a chance. Eddie dropped his eyes. He didn't want to pressure Chris just because he was nice. That made niceness into a handicap too.

"Think about something else," Eddie told himself. He wondered how the dragon was doing in his backpack which he'd ditched next to the door where he could grab it easily on the way into school. "Come on fella, make real magic and help me run," Eddie muttered to himself. Stupid. How was the dragon supposed to do that? Carry him on its back? That'd probably be the only way Eddie would ever run bases fast.

"Eddie," Chris called. And Gary hadn't said anything, at least nothing Eddie had heard. He walked on air as he joined the team. Chris hadn't even picked him last. He'd really run today. He'd fly around those bases.

Darrin was having a fit. Despite his splinted finger, he threw the softball so hard at the ground that it made a dent. "Whaddya pick him for? We're gonna lose for sure now," Darrin screamed at Chris.

Ignoring Darrin, Eddie stood behind Gary who patted him on the shoulder. "Don't worry," Gary said. "We'll win. I feel hot today."

He was too. His turn at bat came, and Gary smacked the ball hard, way into the outfield, and made it all the way to second base. Eddie was so keyed up, his heart beat a tattoo inside his chest.

There were two outs. All he had to do was get to first base and they had a chance of winning. Darrin was on third base, eyeing Eddie hard. He concentrated on how the pitch was coming. With his one-armed hitting, he couldn't get much power, but at least he could connect with the ball.

It came soft and shoulder high. Thwack. Eddie threw himself toward first, determined to get there before they tagged him out. "Come on, Eddie," he heard them yelling. "Come on, come on, you can do it. Run, run." Straining with all his might, Eddie lurched across the spongy field.

"Out," he heard just as he stumbled over the sack that marked the base.

"Out?" he asked in disbelief.

Anita showed him the ball. She'd caught it. Eddie hadn't even known it was on its way. "Jeez," he said.

"I told you not to pick him," Darrin snarled at Chris.

"It's only a game, Darrin," Chris answered.

"But we could've won if you hadn't picked him."

"So we'll win next time," Chris said.

Eddie dripped despair. He couldn't even look up in case he met anybody's eyes. To make it worse the bell rang for the end of the period. Chris put his hand on Eddie's shoulder. "Too bad," he said. "You gave it your best try."

Eddie shrugged and mumbled something. He'd say he didn't feel well and sit out if Chris ever picked him again, rather that than be a burden to a pal.

"Did you see me whack that ball?" Gary asked, catching up with Eddie as they walked back. "I really connected, didn't I?"

"Yeah," Eddie said. "You were good." He hoisted his backpack onto his shoulder. Darrin shoved past him to get inside.

"Hey, Eddie," Darrin said. "You ever see yourself run? This is how you look, Eddie." Darrin lurched through the hallway full of incoming sixth graders who scattered out of his path as he wallowed down the hall like a rowboat in a heavy sea. Nobody laughed at his impersonation, but Eddie felt bad anyway.

"Sic the dragon on him," Gary said angrily. "Now's the time."

Eddie stopped short and closed his eyes concentrating. If he had any control over his blue winged weapon of revenge, now *was* the time to use it. "Get Darrin," Eddie told the dragon out loud. "Go get him."

Nothing happened. They waited until the hall had cleared out, but still nothing happened. "I guess it doesn't work," Eddie said glumly.

Gary sighed. "Yeah, well, that's okay. Listen, he only needs me for an hour after school." "He" was how Gary referred to his father, as if Mr. Winowski were some unnamable, godlike being.

"If you want, I could go to the park with you and Mina."

Gary didn't believe in the dragon anymore, Eddie realized. Well, so what. He didn't really believe in it either. "I'll come by with Mina and wait outside the store for you," Eddie said. He'd bring the dragon along and maybe figure a way to return it to Mr. Winowski instead of knocking himself out to pay for it.

Mina was eager to go to the park. Today she had an adventure in mind. "I'm going to slide down the big slide, Eddie," she told him as they stood outside The Treasure Shop waiting for Gary. She had never dared to go down the big slide, although it tempted her.

"The little slide's fun too," Eddie said, in case she wanted to back out.

Mina nodded. She tipped her head to one side and stuck her lip out as she studied a collection of china dogs in a curio cabinet in the window. Eddie was carrying the dragon in its shoe box. He wondered if he could just leave the shoe box in front of Mr. Winowski's door, as if it were a foundling.

"I have a dollar Walter gave me," Mina said. "Do you think that little dog with the funny face costs more than a dollar, Eddie?"

"What little dog? You mean the one with the freckles?"

"Yes, him. He looks like he needs a home."

The freckle-faced dog was so homely it wasn't likely anyone but Mina would give him a home, Eddie thought, and he said, "We could ask how much it costs."

"Let's. You go and ask that man."

"Mr. Winowski? Are you afraid of him, Mina?"

"Uh huh. He's mean."

"He won't be to customers." Confidently Eddie led Mina inside the store. Gary was nowhere in sight. Mr. Winowski appeared from the depths of the back with a box balanced on his thick shoulders. His glasses magnified his eyes and gave his face a pleasant look, but Eddie wasn't deceived, especially as Mr. Winowski's customer-welcoming smile faded.

"What'da ya want, Eddie? Gary's busy."

"We're customers," Eddie said.

"Yeah? You got money?"

"My little sister wants to see something in the window," Eddie said, ignoring the insulting question.

"What?" Mr. Winowski asked impatiently.

"Show him, Mina," Eddie said. It was discouraging that after nearly four years of being Gary's friend, Mr. Winowski still despised him. Eddie wondered what he'd have to do to change Mr. Winowski's opinion. Become a millionaire doctor and get elected president probably.

Mina turned and walked stiffly out the door. She stood in front of the window waiting. Mr.

Winowski set his box down on a table that so far held only a fancy glass lamp with a fringe of oval crystals hanging from its shade. He walked with shoulders hunched slightly, the way Gary walked.

At the door, Mr. Winowski turned and said to Eddie, "You come out too. I don't want you sticking anything into that pack while I'm not looking."

Eddie gulped, then stood there speechless with shock. Mina was the one who reacted first. "I'm not buying anything from you, you meanie," Mina yelled, and she tried to kick Mr. Winowski, but he backed away from her into his store.

"Get out of here, and take that brat with you," Mr. Winowski shouted. His shout brought Gary from the back at a run.

Just then Eddie felt his backpack jerk. Next thing he knew, the dragon, hawk-size again, was on the floor slithering toward Mr. Winowski who got behind his counter, moving fast. With its wings folded tight as umbrellas along its snaky golden back, the dragon whipped around the counter after the store owner. Mr. Winowski emerged at the other end. He grabbed the box he'd set down and swung it around as if to defend himself with it. Smash went the glass lamp. Its fringe of oval crystals tinkled, falling to the floor.

"Oh boy," Gary said. He stood in back of the store, wide-eyed, watching the commotion.

Mr. Winowski saw his broken lamp and howled. Instantly, Eddie plunged toward the door and Gary followed, propelling him out with a hand on his back.

Without a word, the three of them took off for the park.

"I can't believe it. I can't believe it," Gary kept repeating.

"Can't believe what?" Eddie asked irritably when he'd caught his breath.

"About the dragon. I thought you were kidding. But I saw it."

Eddie reached around with his good arm and pulled the pack off his shoulders. He handed it to Gary. "See if it's still in the shoe box."

It was. "But I saw it," Gary said.

"Me too, and I'm glad our dragon got him," Mina said. "I hate him, after what he said to Eddie."

"He didn't mean it," Gary said. "He had a bad day today. Some old lady walked off with a bunch of silver, and the landlord wants more rent."

"Anyway, I'm still glad," Mina said. "Would you go down the big slide with me, Gary?"

"Sure," Gary said. "You can sit on my lap."

Eddie dropped onto a bench. While Gary followed Mina up the high ladder to the spiral slide, Eddie took the brass body of the dragon out of its tissue paper covering and ran his finger lightly down the scaly back. It felt smooth and cold. The blue wings glistened prettily in the sunlight. So did the red glass eyes. How was it possible that all three of them had seen the dragon come to life? Unless—unless it had really happened.

6

Misunderstood Mina

Eddie woke up with the idea. Immediately, he called Gary, knowing he'd be the one to pick up the phone this early. Mr. Winowski never got up before eight. "Ask him if he saw the dragon," Eddie said as soon as Gary answered.

"Huh?"

"Ask your father—Don't say dragon," Eddie said patiently. "Ask if he saw anything weird yesterday when he broke the lamp."

"He'll get mad if I mention the lamp."

"So, just ask if he saw anything then. Gary, if your *father* saw it, then we know it really happened."

"Oh . . . Yeah . . . Sure." Gary hung up. Eddie

hoped he hadn't gone right back to sleep and forgotten what he was supposed to do.

Breakfast was peaceful that morning. Mom plopped a ladle full of scrambled eggs on Mina's plate and another on Eddie's and then, for a change, sat down to eat with them. She sprinkled black pepper on her own eggs. Mom liked things spicy.

"I've got a dollar and today I'm gonna treat Sara," Mina announced proudly.

"You are?" Mom said. "That's nice, baby."

"What do you want to treat her for?" Eddie asked. "Sara's rich, isn't she?"

"Because she treats, and I never do."

"Umm," Mom said. "Would a quarter a week help?"

Mina's face lit up and she nodded.

Her sudden interest in money reminded Eddie that he needed some too, to pay off his debts. "Eddie," his mother was saying, "I'm going to an all day conference tomorrow. Can you watch Mina for me?"

"Sure," Eddie said. "No problem."

"I want to pay you something. After all, it's the whole day. Would five dollars be too little?"

"More like too much," Eddie said. "You don't have to pay me, Mom."

She knuckled his cheek affectionately. "Listen," she said. "I could never afford what you're worth to me, but don't make me out so poor I can't spare five measly dollars."

Grinning with pleasure at her compliment, Eddie said, "Well, if you really want to—"

"You don't have to pay him, Mama," Mina said. "Eddie *likes* to be with me." Her self-confidence made her brother and mother smile.

As he considered how to earn more than what his mother had promised him, Eddie remembered one of Ms. Kranz's sayings. "The library has the answer to almost any question." He arrived at school early, after his speech therapy session at the Center, and went straight to the library.

"Hi, Ms. Kranz," he greeted the young woman with the long black hair. Today she was wearing a full skirt and heavy Indian jewelry. She usually wore a lot of jewelry. "Got a minute for me?"

"I always have time for you Eddie, love. How's it going?"

"Good, but I need cash. You got anything on how a kid can earn some?"

"I'll bet I do." She led him to the card catalogue. Five minutes later he left with a thick book under his arm. Eddie figured there had to be a good idea somewhere in all those pages.

At lunchtime, Gary said, "Well, I asked him."

"You use the word dragon?"

"No. I did it like you said. Just, 'Did you see anything weird yesterday afternoon?' "

"So what did he say?"

"He said, 'Yeah, your friend Eddie.' But then he asked me what *I* saw. Like maybe he did see something."

"What'd you say?"

"I said I didn't see nothing."

"Uh huh."

"Then he wanted to know what I was asking him for if I didn't see nothing."

"Yeah? So what did you say?"

"I said I was just making conversation."

Eddie chuckled.

"Yeah," Gary nodded smiling. "So he told me I talked too much. I think he's in a better mood because the landlord's not going to raise the rent after all. He's even talking about us going away somewhere for a vacation this summer, like to the mountains for fishing."

"Do you want to?" Eddie asked. He knew he wouldn't. To him, being stuck alone in a cabin in the mountains with Mr. Winowski sounded like the plot of a nightmare. But Eddie knew Gary too well to be surprised by his answer.

"Yeah, it wouldn't be bad, if he was in a good mood. I mean, it's nice going fishing with your father. Know what I mean?"

Eddie knew what he meant, but he thought Gary was dreaming. Mr. Winowski just wasn't that kind of father.

"He's giving me Saturday afternoon off so I can play ball in the park. You want to come?" Gary asked. He meant to watch.

"Sure, if Mina wants to. I'm babysitting her all day."

Eddie found that he'd already tried most of the library book's suggestions for how kids could make money: like getting paid for doing special errands for people, collecting deposit bottles, selling lemonade. And some he couldn't do: like dog walking, being a newspaper boy, shoveling snow, and sitting for neighborhood kids. Mom's five dollars began to look pretty good.

Saturday morning he took the bill his mother handed him, put it in an envelope and wrote on it, "Thanks, Anonymous. Here's your five back. Love, Eddie." He stuck the envelope to the refrigerator with the broken Donald Duck magnet. Now his only debt was for the dragon. Next week he'd try deposit bottle and can collecting again.

"Want to go to the park today?" he asked Mina who was sitting at the kitchen table with her jaw propped between the heels of her hands.

"No. I want Sara to come over."

"Okay. Call and invite her."

"But she won't come."

"Why not?"

"She doesn't like me anymore." Mina's sorrow was strong enough to touch.

"How come? What happened, Mina?"

"Just because I kicked her."

"You kicked her? Mina, I told you Walter was just joking when he said you should kick people. Just because you're small is no excuse."

"Well, but—" Mina said. Her eyes snapped with indignation. "She wouldn't get off the circus pony, and it was *my* turn."

Eddie tried to explain. "You can't go around beating people up just because you're mad at them."

"Why not?"

"Because then they'll be mad at you."

"So what *do* I do then?"

"Well." He considered. "You could have asked her nicely to get off the horse."

"I did."

"And did you tell her she wasn't being fair? Yeah, sure you did. Well, maybe you should've said if she didn't get off the horse, you wouldn't play with her."

"Sara doesn't *want* to play with me anymore."

"Now that," he said, "is a problem."

"See, I told you." After brooding for a minute, Mina suggested they watch television.

By lunchtime, she was weary of cartoons and still glum. Eddie looked in the refrigerator and discovered the weekly food shopping hadn't been done yet. Even the jelly jar was empty. A lonely package of hot dogs sat on an empty shelf. "Want to cook some hot dogs for lunch, Mina?" he asked.

"Okay." She came into the kitchen promptly. He realized she thought he'd meant for her to do the cooking when she said, "You help me, Eddie."

Not wanting to disappoint her, he went along with her role of chief chef. Together they selected the pot. She stood on a chair at the sink to fill it half full of water. He put the pot on the stove for her, and she pushed her chair there and turned on the burner herself.

The phone rang.

"You watch the franks until they're ready, okay?" Eddie said. The phone call was from a friend of his in Administration at the Center for the Disabled. She was calling to invite him to a school party. Once, years ago, she'd brought her grandson in to school to meet him; so now Eddie asked politely about the boy, and she rattled on and on about him.

Eddie noticed that Mina had left her post at the stove. He was still listening to the doting grandma when Mina returned.

"Whew!" he said when he'd hung up. "That lady really can talk."

Mina, back on the chair, had lifted the franks out of the water with a long fork and was busy doing something to them. "Don't look," she said when he got close.

"Why, what are you doing?"

"They busted, and I'm fixing them."

"Fixing what?" Eddie took a step closer just as Tom entered, holding his grease-blackened hands out before him.

"Lemme at the sink, Eddie," Tom said. He turned on the water and looked over Mina's shoulder. "What are you up to, Minnie Mouse?"

"The franks busted. I'm fixing them," Mina said importantly.

Eddie noticed the Band-Aid box just as Tom began to laugh. "You're bandaging the franks?" Eddie asked in disbelief.

Mina ignored him and continued trying to make the Band-Aids stick on the hot, wet franks which had split from overcooking. Eddie snickered. He couldn't help himself.

"What's funny?" Mina demanded, hands on hips as she glared at them.

They explained finally, and she made them apologize for laughing at her. Then they ate the franks. Eddie used ketchup, Tom doused his with mustard, and Mina ate hers plain.

After lunch, Mina's usually expressive face looked pale and blank. "I'm going to find my Bouky," she said. "I think he's tired."

"Sure." Eddie understood. Mina's Bouky was a washed-out stuffed rabbit who'd been her constant companion when she was three. It still served as a comforter when she needed an excuse to take a nap, or when she was sent to her room because her temper had gotten the better of her. Tom was supposed to be the most explosive in the family, but Eddie thought that for her size, Mina was worse. He could remember her turning dark red and howling at her first bath in the kitchen sink when she was just a couple of weeks old. Even Mom had been taken aback at the infant's fury.

Eddie was rinsing the pot, while Tom sat reading Walter's copy of *SPORTS ILLUSTRATED* at the kitchen table, when Mina reappeared.

"I thought you were napping with your Bouky," Eddie said.

Mina looked like a sky set to rain. "I can't find him."

"Want help looking?"

"But I know where he was. I put him to bed in the rag box."

Tom looked up at her. "In the rag box? Why'd you do that?"

"Because it's soft."

"Too bad, Mina. I probably threw him out," Tom said.

Mina gasped.

"Well, I didn't mean to, Min-min. There was a sort of rabbit-like, one eared, faded lump in the rags I took to wash my car. If I'd known it was your Bouky—"

"You threw him out?"

"Listen, I'll buy you a new one."

"I don't *want* a new one," Mina fought against tears but the tears won. "I want my Bouky."

"Hey, cool it," Tom said. "I said I'd get you a better one."

Mina screamed and charged Tom. He caught her hands. She kicked him hard in the shins.

"Ouch! You little brat," Tom said and promptly upended Mina over his knee and spanked her.

"You can't do that. That's Mom's business," Eddie yelled, but his excitement made the words come out mush.

Tom set Mina on her feet. "Now," he said. "I'm not buying you anything until you say you're sorry you kicked me."

"I don't *want* anything from you," Mina screeched and raced out of the room.

"What a little spitfire that kid is," Tom said, rubbing his shin.

"You shouldn't have spanked her," Eddie said. He figured Mina would sleep it off. He'd go up and check on her after she had time to calm down.

A few minutes later Mina marched past them to the kitchen door.

"Good-bye, Eddie," she said. "I forgive you that you laughed at me."

"How long you going to be gone?" he asked her.

"For e-ver." She made it three distinct words. Without a glance at Tom, she took herself and her dolls' clothes suitcase out the back door.

"I guess she's not ready to apologize," Tom said with a grin.

"You better follow her and see where she goes. You walk faster," Eddie said.

"Yeah, okay."

Tom headed for the back door. Anxiously, Eddie warned, "If she sees you following her—"

"Don't worry, she won't," Tom said.

Fifteen minutes later Eddie was fidgeting with nervousness. Mina being Mina, who knew what might happen. Babysitting her hadn't been such a cinch today.

The door opened and Tom sauntered into the kitchen. "She's on her way home. She got to where she had to cross the street, and then couldn't bring herself to ask someone to help her. Maybe she's realizing six is kind of young to make it on her own."

When Mina reentered the kitchen, Tom said, "You're back? Gee, that's too bad."

"Why?" Mina asked.

"Well, 'cause I called Mom and told her to stop by the hospital and bring home a new baby to replace you. How was I to know you were coming back?"

"She's going to get a new baby? Instead of me?"

"Well, you quit the family, didn't you?"

Without warning Mina began to bawl. She bawled so loud and long that she couldn't even hear Eddie telling her that Tom had only been joking.

"What'd you have to be so mean for?" Eddie asked Tom.

tude," Eddie said out loud. "Gravity, gradual, glacial . . ."

He got into bed thinking about the dragon being in Mina's room. Somehow the combination of Mina and the dragon made him uneasy. She was so little, and the dragon got out of hand so easily. There you go again, Eddie chided himself, making it real in your own head. It's just brass and glass. Mina's safe. Just in case though, he got out of bed and crossed the hall to peek into her room. She was sleeping with the shoe box open beside her on the narrow bed. The dragon's blue wings gleamed in the moonlight, glass wings, just brass and glass. Mina was fine.

Eddie yawned sleepily and shuffled back to his own bed.

7

It Really Works

Mina had afternoon kindergarten classes. Mornings, the lady next door watched her after Mom went to work. Since Mina didn't like the lady next door much, she usually slept late and turtled her way over there as slowly as possible. That's why Eddie was surprised to see her scoot out of their house as he stood waiting for the school bus. She came churning down the sidewalk and thrust the shoe box that held the dragon at him.

"How come you're in such a hurry to give him back?" Eddie asked her.

"Because I made him get Tom already."

"How?"

"He *bleeded*, Eddie." She sounded upset.

"Tom?"

She nodded. "I sicced him on Tom in the garage

the class about the importance of homework, and how it was all for their own good so they'd succeed in high school and college and life, and how hard she worked trying to improve them, and how the least they could do was—"Eddie," she snapped. "Stop what you're doing and pay attention to me."

"I'm looking for my homework," he said.

"Of course you are," she mocked him. "And in a minute now, you'll tell me you must have left it home."

"I might have."

"What?"

"Maybe I did leave it home, Miss Clark, but I did do it," he said.

Miss Clark looked blank.

"He says he did it, but he left it home, Miss Clark," a helpful classmate interpreted for him.

"That isn't even an original excuse," Miss Clark said. Her eyes darted glances around the room, stinging here and there with dislike. Finally she returned to Eddie, and the dislike condensed into pure hatred.

"All right," she said, "if you've done your homework, let's hear you correct the paragraph." The air crackled as she whipped around on her high heels and began copying the incorrect paragraph onto the blackboard.

"Stand up, Eddie," she commanded, "and start."

He got to his feet. Sympathetic faces turned his

way. He smiled to reassure them. It was okay. He could do it. He'd had Tom check the work for him last night, and Tom had straightened him out on the only two errors he'd made.

The sentences on the board so far read:

> The boys is jumping up and down with joy because they is going on a vacation at a cottage where they was last summer. Bob's dog do not want to go with he in the car because Bob's dog do not like to ride in the car with his sister's cat. Her tells the dog to come to she.

"Ahem," Eddie began, delighted to prove Miss Clark in the wrong for a change. Too bad Gary wasn't there to witness this. "The boys *are* jumping up and down with joy because they *are* going—"

"What?" Miss Clark interrupted. "Slow down so that the class can understand you, Eddie."

Eddie began again slowly.

"They *are* going," Miss Clark said, repeating his words. "The subject is plural and the verb must agree with it—not is, but are."

"That's what Eddie said," a boy called out.

"Raise your hand when you have something to say," Miss Clark snapped. "Continue, Eddie."

He mouthed every word carefully getting his tongue around it so that she'd understand him, but her eyes kept scanning the room in pursuit of the spitballers and note passers, and it didn't seem that she was paying attention to him. ". . . they *were* last summer . . ." He was one sentence short of finishing when she interrupted him.

"Who can correct what Eddie's said so far?" Miss Clark asked.

Nobody raised a hand. There was nothing to correct. Miss Clark insisted, "It won't help not to cooperate. Unless you want to be tested on this today . . . How many of you are ready for a test on this subject?"

No hands. No one wanted to fall into whatever trap she was setting for them.

"Well then, let's hear the paragraph read correctly. Elise."

Elise, tall, thin and meek, stood up and began whispering her way rapidly through the paragraph exactly as Eddie had read it.

"Sit down, Eddie," Miss Clark said. "You're excused."

"*You're* not," Eddie shot back. In his fury at her, he was talking back to a teacher for the first time in his life, but there was no excuse for what she'd done to him.

Now she understood him. "Eddie, you march yourself down to the office and wait there until I get to you," Miss Clark spluttered.

Anger broke down all his carefully built-up muscle control, and Eddie knocked over a chair in his awkward attempt to collect his belongings. Miss Clark gasped as if he had done it deliberately.

Just then Gary ambled into the classroom late, his usual apologetic grin in place. He held his pass out at arm's length as if Miss Clark might bite when she took it.

"Gary, you take Eddie down to the principal's office," she said, yanking the pass out of his hand. "You've already missed most of the period anyway."

"Sure, Miss Clark," Gary said and cheerfully went to help Eddie pick up the books he'd scattered in his agitation. Holding the books under one arm, Gary guided Eddie out of the room with the other.

When they were alone in the hall, Gary asked, "So what happened?"

Eddie was too shaken to speak. Finally he got enough control of himself to say, "I had it right." Then he called Miss Clark the private, nasty nickname her students had started using for her after the end of the early fall honeymoon period, when everyone had liked her because she was young. Applied to a female dog, the word was correct.

"Boy, I never seen you this mad," Gary said.

"Saw," Eddie corrected him. "She should've had that too. Seen and saw. I know those too, but she won't believe I know anything."

"Hey, slow down. I don't get what you're saying."

When he finally understood what had happened, Gary said, "So what's the big deal? You know she's a bozo. I bet most of the kids in the class know you were right, and you know it. So?"

"So how am I going to get to college? How am I going to be a psychologist if they can't figure out what I'm telling them?" Eddie demanded shrilly.

"You're going too fast again, Eddie," Gary said.

Eddie thought he was kidding and socked him. Gary let himself be socked. He was used to being a punching bag for overcharged people. His father sometimes hit him too.

"Okay," Eddie said. "That's it. I'll sic the dragon on her. She'll see."

"Huh? The dragon? You got him with you?"

For an answer, Eddie pulled the dragon out of the box in his pack. He held the sinewy brass body in his shaking hands. A tingle went up his arm, as if the dragon were infusing him with strength. "You get Miss Clark. You get her good," Eddie told the dragon.

Gary's eyes widened. Both he and Eddie held their breaths watching. The blue glass wings quivered slightly but remained brittle glass.

"What a handsome piece, Eddie!" It was the art teacher with the big blue eyes whom everybody loved. She'd come up the hall toward them silently on her rubber soles. "Is it yours?"

Eddie nodded.

"Beautiful workmanship. I'd love to make a slide of it for a class I teach. Would you lend it to me just for a period? I'll give it back after lunch."

Wordlessly, Eddie handed over the dragon.

"Thanks," she said. "You're a darling." And off she went in the blue smock that matched her eyes.

"What'd you do that for?" Gary asked. "I thought you wanted to get Miss Clark?"

"I don't know," Eddie said. "She asked me; so I just—Come on, Gare. We better get to the office before Miss Clark does."

A lecture and loss of recess for the rest of the week was Eddie's punishment for his two word display of temper. Miss Clark told him to sit out the recesses in the library. He couldn't believe his luck. Normally he never got enough time in the library. He was so pleased he almost made the mistake of thanking her.

The art teacher didn't return the dragon after lunch, but Eddie didn't worry. His dragon was in good hands, and meanwhile his anger was shrinking to a less painful lump.

He turned down the hall to the library as his classmates crowded out the double doors from the cafeteria to the field to play softball. Anita Valdez walked out of the girls' room as he passed it.

"Eddie," she said. "I'm sorry. We should have—*I* should have told Miss Clark you did the paragraph perfectly this morning. That was so rotten. I did put a note on her desk about it though."

"Thanks," Eddie said. He smiled at Anita. She smiled back and was gone before he could think of a more witty reply. Trust his brain to shut down just when he needed it. He was still smiling as he walked into the library.

"Eddie! Did the book help?" Ms. Krantz asked.

"Not me. I'm still in debt," he said.

"Well, I just put up a poster that might interest you." She steered him to it. The P.T.A. was sponsoring a school-wide contest for library week with a prize of ten dollars for the best composition on "Why I Love Books." The composition would be read aloud by the author in assembly at the end of the month.

"What do you think?" Ms. Krantz asked.

"Not a chance. Not for me," Eddie said.

"Why not? You like to read, and you can write, can't you?"

"Not enough to win a prize." It wasn't his writing ability he doubted so much as his speaking ability. He could never read a speech aloud in assembly. No way.

As if she were reading his mind, Ms. Krantz added, "And if you win and don't want to read your composition yourself, I'm sure they'd let someone do it for you." She zipped her eyebrows up and down humorously. "I'm sure because I'm one of the judges."

Her encouragement pleased Eddie so much that he promised to think it over. It was the least he could do in response to her kindness.

At the end of the day, Eddie detoured past the art room to reclaim his dragon which he figured the art teacher had forgotten to return. She nearly bumped into him coming out of her room. She was holding the dragon.

"Eddie, I would have returned this when I promised, but I had to drive poor Miss Clark home. Sorry."

"Miss Clark?"

"Didn't you hear what happened to her? She went out to her car and caught her heel on the curb. She may have broken something in her foot. I expect she'll be out for a while."

"She broke her foot?" Eddie was awed. He'd told the dragon to get her, yes, but he hadn't meant to do her that much harm. "Gee, I'm sorry," Eddie said, feeling guilty.

"You're *such* a nice boy." The blue eyes admired him warmly. "A lot of kids cheered when they heard about Miss Clark."

The dragon was warm from the art teacher's hands. Eddie tucked it inside his shirt and stuffed the shirt back in his pants. That was faster than getting the pack off his back, undoing it and laying the dragon in its shoe box, and he had a bus to catch.

All the way home, the dragon purred peacefully, tickling Eddie's ribs as he sat beside Mina on the bus. Mina was quietly looking out the window while Eddie mulled over the strange happenings of the day. Having a pet dragon was an advantage, certainly, especially a dragon that could be carried around in a shoe box and taken to school. But he had to get his dangerous pet under control. Just a little nip or scare was enough to even up the score with an enemy. Blood and broken bones were wrong, very, very wrong.

"What we gotta do is tame you," Eddie told his dragon.

"Me?" Mina asked him.

"Not you," Eddie said. "The dragon."

"Dragons can't be tamed," Mina said. "People got to kill them."

"No!" Eddie protested and put his hand protectively against the lump in his shirt. Nothing was going to happen to his dragon. The poor guy was just doing his job the best way he knew how. It wasn't his fault people got hurt worse than they should. Problems, Eddie thought. As soon as he got one out of the way, another came along. He sighed and Mina leaned her head against his shoulder.

"Don't feel bad, Eddie," she said. "I'm here."

"Yeah," he said, and despite his worry, a smile perked up the corners of his mouth.

8

Going It Alone

Sure enough, Miss Clark was absent the next day. They had a male sub who was almost as strict. No one would say exactly what she'd broken, but the rumor was she had a cast on her foot. Eddie spent the day thinking about the essay contest. The ten dollar prize, added to what he already had, would get him out of debt. He'd left his dragon home for safekeeping, but the art teacher sent him a message that her slides hadn't come out, and she'd appreciate it if he'd give her another chance at photographing his dragon.

Back to school Friday morning went the dragon. It didn't seem to mind. That evening, Eddie brought Gary home with him so they could do their social studies homework.

"Where were you kids?" Martin demanded.

"Mom had to leave for her bowling league. You were supposed to be home an hour ago."

"We were in the park," Eddie said, "and nobody had a watch."

"They were giving me batting practice," Gary said.

"I'm X-austed," Mina said, using the big word so dramatically that even Martin smiled. At least, the corner of his mouth twitched.

"Mina chased balls for us," Gary explained.

"It's okay if Gary eats with us, Martin, isn't it?" Eddie asked.

Martin shrugged. "Mom left a pot of stew. There's plenty, but you guys better clean up after yourselves. I'm going out."

"You got a date tonight?" Gary asked.

Martin disliked personal questions. He gave Gary a sour look and Eddie asked quickly, "Where's Tom?"

"At Joe's working on his car. Where else?" Martin said. He bumped the table and knocked Eddie's backpack off it on the way out.

Eddie yelped. Hastily he opened the backpack and checked out the shoe box. The dragon was undamaged.

"What are you carrying that thing around for?" Martin asked.

"That's Eddie's pet dragon," Gary said. "It protects him."

"Come on!" Martin said to Gary "*You* might be

nuts enough to believe in magic, but Eddie's too hard-headed."

"It *is* magic," Mina assured Martin. "It does things."

"What things?" Martin asked.

"It bites people."

Martin laughed out loud. "I bet," he said and winked at Eddie, in the certainty that Eddie was on his wave-length. "Okay, you kids, behave yourselves. I've got to get going."

"Have fun," Gary called after him. "Whoever she is."

"Teasing Martin about girls makes him mad," Eddie told Gary when the back door had shut.

Eddie handed down the dinner plates to Mina who set the table for the three of them. Gary got the knives and forks from the drawer. "There's nothing in the house for dessert, Gare," Eddie said.

"That's okay. My father got a bucket of wings on sale. Every night this week we've been eating chicken. One more wing and I'll fly away." Gary flapped his elbows, squawking like a remarkably loud chicken.

Eddie smiled absently at Gary's attempt at humor. "Hey Gary, you know that essay contest? If I win, would you read it in assembly for me?"

"You mean like an announcer? I was an announcer in the play last year, remember? And once I was a bear. That was in first grade. Only I knocked the tree over. That was pretty funny."

"So you'd do it for me?"

"Sure." He stood up and shouted, "Four score and seven years ago—"

"That hurts my ears," Mina said as she covered them with her hands.

Gary settled down to eat the generous portion of stew that Eddie had ladled onto his plate. "You get any ideas yet, Eddie?"

"I'm going to work on it this weekend." Monday was the deadline. Eddie figured it shouldn't take him more than a few hours once he got started. He cut the lone piece of beef on his plate small enough to swallow without chewing. Mostly what he'd served himself was gravy with onions and carrots and potatoes.

"Yum. Your Mom makes great stew," Gary said.

"Maybe the dragon wants some," Mina murmured as she poked her food around her plate.

"The dragon's dead, Mina. He doesn't need to eat," Gary said.

"He's dead?" Mina looked alarmed.

"Well, he's not alive. So he don't need to eat like us," Gary explained.

"Yes, he *is* alive sometimes," Mina said. "He moves. We seed him, didn't we?"

"Yeah, but—Eddie, you tell her."

"The dragon doesn't need food or sleep because he's not flesh and blood like us. He's a different kind of thing."

"Like he can bite people," Mina said.

"I don't know," Eddie said. "We never saw him bite, did we? I think he just scares people."

"When he gets mad," Mina said.

"Well, I'm not sure he gets mad exactly. He probably doesn't have feelings like people do," Eddie said. He touched the dragon which was lying in its box on the table next to him. It felt cold and hard. But at night, when it snuggled up and made a rumbling noise, then it certainly seemed to have feelings—or was that only in Eddie's dreams?

"Glass and metal can't feel," Eddie said as surely as if Martin were looking over his shoulder.

"How do you know?" Mina asked.

"Well, because—" Eddie thought about it. "Because you don't—because it isn't alive, like us. If you break it, it doesn't bleed."

"When Mama unwrapped the stew meat, I saw blood," Mina said. "Was it alive?"

"Not in the package. But when it was an animal, it was. To be alive, I guess it's got to move and grunt. Not just bleed."

She looked at him suspiciously. "Trees are alive though."

His jaw dropped. "Mina, you're too smart. Yeah, trees are alive. I think. I mean they grow so—"

"And they don't grunt."

Gary started chuckling. He'd already finished what was on his plate. According to Gary, he and his father never spent more than ten minutes on a meal. They were super-speed eaters.

"I give up," Eddie said. "You answer her, Gary."

"Let's play Chinese Checkers," Gary said. "Or better yet, me and Mina can play Chinese Checkers, and you and the dragon can do the dishes."

"Dragons can't do dishes," Mina informed him.

"Why not?" Gary asked with mock surprise.

"Because they're not supposed to."

"I think she knows more about dragons than we do, Eddie," Gary said. They did the dishes together, the three of them. Then they played Chinese Checkers. The dragon stayed on the table without participating.

That night Eddie dreamed again. He heard the dragon shuffling around his bedroom. Its wings made a strange hollow racket as they rubbed against each other.

"What's the matter?" Eddie whispered. He didn't expect an answer.

"Come here," Eddie coaxed. The wings flapped dryly and then came the delicate touch of the narrow head as it slipped into the hollow of Eddie's neck where it just fit. The purr, when it finally came, had a skipped beat that was new.

"You feeling bad about something?" Eddie asked. Gently he stroked the silky body resting so trustingly against his. A great sadness came from the dragon, like body heat. "Hey," Eddie said. "You got troubles, fella? You want to get out of being who you are sometimes, too?"

Eddie shivered as the dragon moved away from him, leaving a cold spot where the warm had been. "Don't go away. Don't leave me," Eddie begged and woke up.

There stood his mother touching his head.

"You all right, honey? You're having a dream."

"Umm," Eddie said sleepily. "How was your bowling league, Mom?"

"Good. We won." She bent her ample body to kiss him, and he fell back asleep.

Gary had to work that Saturday, and Mina had been invited to go to Sara's parents' camp with them. Sara and Mina were friends again. Mina kept running up and down the stairs in her excitement—to get a ball to bring with her, back up for the sweater Mom said she might need in the mountains, up again to go to the bathroom, and one last time to change her tee shirt after she spilled her juice on it.

"They better pick her up soon or she'll wear herself out," Eddie said to Mom.

"She didn't eat her breakfast," Mom fretted. "I'll pack some crackers and fruit, and she can share them with Sara in the car."

"Mina throws up if she eats in a car. You want her throwing up on Sara?"

"No, that's right," Mom said. She dithered over the fruit and finally let Mina go without it when Sara's father honked for her.

"Give me a kiss," Mom said as Mina stood poised to run out the door.

Mina kissed her, then backtracked to hug and kiss Eddie too. "Don't miss me too much, Eddie," she said.

Eddie and Mom had a good laugh over that one after Mina had gone. "Isn't she something!" Mom said. "Well, what are you doing today?"

"Writing my prize-winning composition on why I love books. Any ideas, Mom?"

"Not me. Ask one of your brothers. I wasn't the greatest in English."

"What are *you* doing today?" Eddie asked.

"Visiting my friend who's laid up. I want to see what I can do for the poor soul. She lives by herself. Want to come with me?"

"No thanks. I've got that composition, and then I'm going to look for more deposits in the woods."

"Alone? I don't like you going into the woods alone, Eddie."

"I'm not a baby, Mom."

"Ummm." She frowned and said reluctantly, "Well, I guess I can't keep you wrapped in cotton wool all your life, can I?"

She left finally, and he had the house to himself. He settled down at the kitchen table with his spiral notebook and pen to wait for inspiration. None came. He began writing anyway. "Books come in all different shapes and sizes. Some are full of pictures, and some have mostly words. They can teach you things and make you laugh." Boring he decided, reading over what he'd written. It had to be special or forget it, he'd never win.

"So what is a book?" he wrote. Not bad, kind of catchy for a first line. Only next he had to answer his own question. "It's paper and print, but it's more also. It's facts and ideas and make believe." There he went, listing again. Listing was dull, dull, dull.

He remembered the book Mina had made Mom check out of the library for her over and over again when she was two or three. It was a tiny book by the lady who wrote Peter Rabbit a hundred years ago, and the words were much too hard for Mina to understand, but she carried it with her everywhere. Eddie had never figured out why. Eventually Mina made up her own story as she turned the pages, a story that had nothing to do with the pictures of mice in the book. Strange.

No stranger than his invention of a pet dragon though. And if the little sister he was closer to than anyone was a mystery to him, how did he expect to understand his own mind? Imagine him inventing a dragon that purred, glass and brass that came to life! If Martin knew, he'd be positive Eddie was crazy.

Eddie put down his pen and shoved the spiral

notebook aside. He wasn't in the mood for thinking. He wanted to be Eddie, the hard-headed realist, the kid whom Martin respected. What he'd do was take himself up to the woods now to look for deposits. That was real and simple enough. As for the dragon, his so-called "protection," naturally, he'd leave it behind.

Eddie rounded up two plastic garbage bags from under the kitchen sink and set off for the woods. There hadn't been much rain, and it was dry underfoot as he crunched over dead leaves. Overhead, the space was filled with feathery leaves that filtered the sunlight greenly. No birds sang in the noon lull. It felt as if he had the woods all to himself, but there had been a party in the clearing recently. Eddie saw signs of a fire. He wondered how they dared to make a fire when the smoke would be certain to bring the police up here.

An hour of scrabbling around the clearing resulted in half a garbage bag full of deposits. Not bad, but he needed to do better.

He started down the path to Darrin's shack, hoping the gang might have pitched their empties nearby. On the way he stopped and listened to be certain he was alone. If Darrin and his buddies happened to be using the shack—No, it was too quiet. Just leaves rustling. Wind sifting through the branches. Eddie kept going.

He was startled a few seconds later when Darrin's buddy, Mack, stepped from behind a tree into the path five feet ahead. Mack was zipping his fly as if he'd just relieved himself. "What are you doing here?" he demanded. The very lack of expression in his good-looking face made it somehow menacing.

"Nothing."

"You spying on us?"

"You crazy? What'd I want to spy on you for?"

"Then what're you here for?"

The plastic garbage bag pressed into Eddie's good shoulder. He almost showed its contents, but hesitated. Mack was sure to confiscate the deposits, especially since Eddie had already done the hard work of collecting them.

"What you got in that bag?" Mack asked.

"Garbage. I'm cleaning up the woods."

"Yeah? Let me see."

"Why should I?" Eddie asked as he backed up. He considered trying to knock Mack off balance by swinging the bag at him and then running, but he knew he wouldn't get very far the way he ran.

Suddenly Mack reached forward and yanked the bag out of Eddie's hand, practically pulling his shoulder out of its socket in the process.

"Deposits," Mack said. "Say, were *you* the kid who stole ours? . . . you come with me. Darrin wants to see *you*." Mack grabbed Eddie's arm and hauled him along the path toward the shack. Eddie struggled but Mack didn't seem to notice. At least, he didn't slow down any.

"Ouch," Eddie yelled when a branch got him in the cheek. "Watch it, you jerk. You wanna poke my eye out?"

"You'll get worse when Darrin sees who was messing around in our hideout."

The dragon, Eddie thought as cold fear trickled through his veins. He should have brought his dragon. Without it, he was done for.

9

Helpless

The mismatched boards and patches of building material that formed the roof of the hideout had been pulled aside to expose the entrance.

"Did you find any beer?" It was Darrin's voice from the dark cavity below.

Mack leaned over the opening, his fingers a vise on Eddie's good arm. "Nah, but look what I found instead." Mack yanked his prisoner closer and shoved Eddie's head down. Eddie smelled smoke and looked down into Darrin's broad flat face. A cigarette jutted from his mouth. Slowly, the cigarette moved up and then down as Darrin's mean eyes fixed on Eddie. Darrin didn't move from the old car seat which was pulled up to a table below the hole. On a stool across from him, Richard perched like a chicken hawk alert for the attack.

Smoke from the candle burning in the center of the table made Eddie's eyes smart.

"What're you doing here, Eddie, spying on us?" Darrin asked.

"He's collecting deposits," Mack said before Eddie could answer. "He's the one stole ours, I bet."

"A thief?" Darrin showed his teeth in a smile. "Nah, not old Eddie. He's a good boy. Aren't you a good boy, Eddie?"

Eddie clamped his mouth shut.

"Heave him down here, Mack, so we can look him over," Darrin ordered.

Abruptly, Eddie found himself hanging head first above the table. Mack had hold of his heels. The blood rushed to his head. Pain shot through his left leg, and he screamed or tried to, but his tongue stuck in the back of his throat. He began choking. The candle flame wavered practically under his nose as he twisted around to get loose.

"His hair's catching fire," Richard said.

The next thing Eddie knew, he was slung upright against the wall, and Darrin's hands, with the splinted finger, were rubbing Eddie's head hard. Eddie's bad leg buckled and he slumped to the floor.

The silence that followed was broken by thumps as Mack jumped to the table and then to the floor. Three expressionless faces contemplated Eddie like Halloween masks in the gloom. He tried to control his breathing, determined not to reveal his fear.

"The thing is," Darrin said conversationally, "it

doesn't really matter if he's a thief or not. Now he knows where our hideout is, we got to do something about him."

"I knew before and I didn't tell," Eddie blurted out. He had to repeat himself twice before Darrin consented to understand him.

"So you didn't tell? Well, that's nice, Eddie, but how do we know you won't now? Also," Darrin said self-righteously, "Mack says you stole our deposit cans, and we can't let you get away with that, can we?"

"You stole money from me," Eddie said. "We're even."

Darrin frowned. "You calling me a thief, Eddie?" He was the picture of the honest citizen as he stood there straight-backed and serious.

"I'm not calling you anything," Eddie said. "Just let me go home."

"I don't see how we can do that." Darrin shook his head with regret. He seemed to be pitying Eddie for what was going to happen to him.

Eddie shivered.

"We could make him swear not to tell," Richard suggested. The prospect of hurting Eddie obviously made Richard nervous.

"Yeah, we could do that, but I don't know," Darrin said thoughtfully. "Squeeze his arm back a little, Mack. Let's hear how good he swears."

Mack obliged promptly. He yanked Eddie's

good arm up behind his back and pushed on it until Eddie screamed.

"You ready to swear you'll never give away our secret hideout?" Darrin asked.

"I was ready before you hurt me," Eddie yelled. Then because they continued to stare at him, he said slowly, "I won't tell."

Darrin yawned and stubbed out his cigarette. "See," he told Mack and Richard, "making him promise is easy. But how're we going to be sure he keeps his promise? Now how about that?"

"I keep my promises," Eddie said.

Darrin ignored him. "And we can't let him get away with robbing us. That wouldn't be right. I say we tie him up and leave him here while we go home and think this thing out carefully. What do you say, Richard?"

Richard shrugged.

"Mack?"

"Whatever you say, Darrin."

"Okay, then tie him up." Darrin sat down again, propped his workboots one over the other on the table, and shook another cigarette out of the pack.

Richard got a piece of nylon clothesline from a box under the table. Mack helped him tie Eddie's hands behind his back. With the leftover rope end, they tied his feet together for good measure. The position hurt.

"Hey," Eddie said as they all three gathered

around the table, "you don't have to tie me up. I can't get out of here on my own. Come on, give me a break. My arms are killing me."

They ignored him and sat quietly smoking as if they had all the time in the world. "Come on, guys," Eddie begged as he writhed in an effort to relieve the tension on his muscles. "Give me a break. I never did anything to you." Silence. Desperately he offered, "You can keep all the deposits I picked up today, and I'll get more for you whenever you want."

"Shut up, Eddie, or we'll have to gag you," Darrin said.

Eddie whimpered. He couldn't help himself. The pain was bad, and he couldn't escape it. Fiercely he shook his head and tried to spit, but his mouth was dry and his tongue felt swollen.

"By the way, was he out there alone?" Darrin asked Mack.

"I think so."

"He's always got Gary or his little sister with him. You're sure they're not going for help?"

"I didn't hear anybody talking." Mack's face was set on neutral.

Eddie wondered what would make Mack nervous. "My brothers will be looking for me," he said. "I'm supposed to be home. They'll come looking for me any minute."

"Yeah?" Darrin said coolly. "Probably not. Probably they're glad to be rid of you. But we'd better gag you so nobody hears you yelling down here."

"No," Eddie said. "I won't yell, Darrin. Hey, please!"

It took them a while to figure out what to use as a gag. Finally they untied Eddie's hands, pulled off his nylon jacket and used that. Then they retied his hands. One after the other, the three of them climbed from a ladder on the table up through the roof. Then they slid the board over the hole.

In the sudden dimness, the candle drew Eddie's eyes. He thought of all the TV shows where people got themselves untied. If he could roll himself over to the table and get to his feet somehow, he could lean close enough to the flame for it to burn the line connecting his feet to his hands. A lot of ifs he told himself, too many even for a kid who didn't have C.P. If only he'd brought his dragon! How long would Darrin leave him here? Eddie shuddered and moaned. His brothers would come and search the woods. Sure, but when? And would they find the hideout? Suppose they didn't. He could die here. No, that was ridiculous. Darrin wouldn't kill him. He was too smart to go that far. Wasn't he? That kid whose body was found in the woods last year— no, someone would come eventually. Darrin was mean but not crazy. Eddie just had to wait out the pain and eventually—

Mom, Eddie thought. He'd told her he was going to the woods. Maybe she'd come home early and—but she wouldn't send one of his brothers after him unless he was very late. That would be hours from now. It was chilly. Only the pain was hot and throbbing.

"Calm down," Eddie told himself. "Calm down and try to help yourself."

He let himself slide onto the damp dirt floor, booby-trapped with tree roots and rocks and who knew what kind of filth. Still, rolling over to the table was easier than he'd thought. Getting upright again, once he'd reached it, was harder. He had to ignore the pain and use muscles that he'd never tried before. In desperation, he turned around and managed to grasp the table leg backwards with his good right hand. Pushing against the table leg helped. Only while he was pulling himself upright, he jiggled the table and the candle flame went out.

Rats. It was dark as a coffin without the candle. Worse than a coffin, it was like being in the grave itself. The dank air smelled foul.

"Don't panic," he told himself. "Think. Think. There has to be something." If he could find the matches— It was an impossible idea, but better attempt it than stand there shivering in terror.

He recalled the box under the table that Mack had taken the rope from. Would they keep matches too? It meant getting down to the floor again.

Eddie almost gave up because it had been so hard to raise himself upright, but then he didn't give up. He hit his head on the corner of the table lowering himself to the floor. Next he inched backward until his fingers touched the box. Wriggling, by some miracle, he got his good hand loose. For a minute he rested. Then he poked weakly in the box and felt the metal container of matches. He tore at the gag which he'd forgotten in his anxiety to find the matches, dropped the matches, couldn't get the knot untied, and finally did. At last, he worked the rope loose from his ankles and stood up with the matches in his hands.

Good, but now he had to urinate. All the excitement, in addition to not having relieved his bladder since breakfast, was having its effect. Serve them right if he did it right there next to their table. Except he didn't want to. He thought of the humiliating accidents he used to have at the Center when he was six and seven. He wasn't giving Darrin a chance to sneer at him for that on top of everything else.

"Help," he yelled in frustration. "Help."

A square of light appeared above him as the boards were removed. Darrin's face, squared by his grin, floated in the opening. Immediately, the grin faded. "You got loose? How'd you do that, Eddie?"

Eddie froze. They'd tie him up again for sure. "I gotta go pee," he said.

Darrin's eyebrows went up. "You better not do it there," he said. "Stink up our place and you'll make me mad."

"I've gotta *go*, Darrin."

Darrin's head disappeared, and there was a whispered conference above. Then Mack jumped down, making the table shake. He lifted Eddie, and Darrin grabbed him and pulled him the rest of the way.

"Okay," Darrin said. "So go."

Eddie turned to move off into the trees.

"Oh, no you don't. Think you're going to get away from us?"

"I can't get away. You can run faster than me any day," Eddie said angrily. He wriggled while Darrin considered, and Richard and Mack snickered at Eddie's predicament. Suddenly Eddie's bladder made its own decision. Hot urine ran down his leg, soaking his soft, faded jeans.

They roared as if it were the funniest thing they'd ever seen. While Eddie stood there in an agony of embarrassment, they hooted and called him a baby, a sissy. He felt like crying. Worse than the pain was the helplessness.

"Ah, maybe we oughta let the poor cripple go," Darrin said. "What do you think guys? We got something on him now. He tells, and we tell how Eddie still wets his pants like a baby."

Rage burned away Eddie's embarrassment.

"See," Darrin said, making a sweeping bow to invite Eddie to leave. "See what nice guys we are? We didn't do a thing to you, did we, Eddie?"

Losing his temper entirely, Eddie started calling them all the names he could think of. They didn't react. Either they didn't understand him, or they didn't care what he said.

Darrin took him by the shoulders. "Now listen," he said earnestly. "Anyone messes up our hideout and we know who to blame. You get me? And next time, we won't be so nice."

Eddie stumbled down the path, banging into rocks and tree branches until he reached the road. An old woman watched him curiously as he headed home past her picket fence, twitching, aching, afraid of collapsing on the street. All that held him up was his fury. He'd shamed himself before those hoods. Darrin had shoved him right back into infanthood. He'd kill them, Eddie vowed. He'd make them sorry they'd done this to him.

He was too exhausted to get the back door of his house open. Tom opened it after Eddie'd banged on it for a while.

"What's the matter with you, forget your key?"

"Get out of my way," Eddie said. He wanted to get upstairs and change before anyone saw him, but Tom was too quick.

"What's the matter, you couldn't find a bush?"

Red-faced, Eddie made it to the stairs. He dragged himself up, half crawling, and got himself into his room. There he got out of his wet, dirty clothes. Finally, he rolled into bed shivering, with barely enough energy to reach out and gather the dragon to him from where he'd left it on the night table.

"Get those guys," Eddie ordered hoarsely. "You get them and make them sorry."

The smooth brass body flexed under his fingers.

The red eyes glittered, reflecting Eddie's fury. Rapidly the dragon expanded. Blue wings unfolded like great sails in the shadowy twilight, until with a whoosh of wings, the dragon flew out the open window into the early dark.

Eddie slept.

"Are you coming down for dinner, honey?" his mother asked, her hand cool on his brow.

"Too tired."

"Are you all right?"

"Um humm."

"Tom said you seemed upset."

"I'm all right."

"What happened to you today?"

"Nothing. . . . Did Mina have a good time with Sara?"

"Oh, sure. She can't wait to tell you about it."

"Tomorrow," he murmured. His mother took the dragon from his hand and set it back on the night table. Eddie fell back to sleep.

In his dream he saw the flames. The dragon hovered like a great eagle over the shack on the hill, feeding the flames with his fiery breath and the beat of his blue wings. In Eddie's dream everything was hot and angry and red. Revenge felt good.

10

Another Way Out

Eddie first heard about the fire Sunday morning. His brothers were talking about it at breakfast. "I saw it," Walter said, "from the bowling alley parking lot. The whole sky was lit up by the flames from those woods. I can't believe you slept right through it, Tom."

Mom was at the stove, making pancakes to add to the stack that was rapidly disappearing from the platter on the table. Eddie sat down next to Martin, across from Tom and Mina. "What woods burned up?" Eddie asked.

"Our woods. Where the climbing tree is—was," Walter said. "There's nothing but black stumps and smoke left this morning."

"Thank God it didn't happen during the day,"

Mom said. "Weren't you there yesterday looking for deposit bottles, Eddie?"

He nodded and looked over Martin's shoulder at the front page of the local Sunday paper. It featured a big photograph of firemen shooting water at the picket fence and little house at the foot of the hill.

"You don't know anything about the fire, do you, Eddie?" Martin asked.

"No," Eddie said. He thought of Darrin's hide-out and the candle and the cigarettes. Then he remembered the dragon and the dream he'd had last night. No, he told himself. No, it couldn't be.

"I used to party there all the time," Walter said regretfully. "I kissed my first girl in those woods."

"And we played Indians, and cops and robbers," Tom said. "Remember when I fell out of the climbing tree?"

"Well, it's gone," Martin said. "According to this article, the whole hill went, and they were just lucky to save the houses nearby."

"Eddie and me liked the woods too," Mina said. Her agile tongue licked leftover syrup from the tip of her spoon.

Eddie speared a pancake, resisting the guilt pushing in on him. Come on, he told himself, you didn't set that fire. You don't even own a match.

He did, however, own the dragon, and yesterday he'd sicced it on Darrin, and last night he'd had the dream. He'd *seen* the fire in that dream. But it was crazy to think his dragon could have started a fire. It had to have been the cigarettes or the candle. Except, where had the dream come from?

"How come you're so quiet this morning, Eddie?" Mom wanted to know.

"He feels bad about the woods," Walter said sympathetically.

Eddie didn't feel well. He still ached from yesterday's struggles, but he didn't want to talk about it. They'd feel sorry for him, and then he'd feel worse. Also, he didn't want his brothers getting after Darrin and his gang. It was enough that Darrin had probably lost his hideout.

After breakfast, Mom and Mina went to church with Martin, while Tom and Walter worked on the yard, cutting and raking and mowing. Eddie dragged himself up the road to see what the fire had done. To his surprise, he found Gary there gawking at the hill.

"Hey, Eddie. Isn't this something!" Gary stood with his hands on his hips looking up at the still smoking hillside which was now shades of black and gray and brown. The old three-speed he'd used to get there was propped against a corner of the charred picket fence. Green still showed on some upper branches of the largest trees on the hill, but all the underbrush had been burned away, and most trees were burned stumps. "Guess we won't be collecting deposits here no more."

The devastation made Eddie feel sick.

"The fire trucks woke me up last night," Gary

said. "Did you hear them? They went right by our house and woke me up. Rrrrang, Rrrrrang." Gary's imitation of sirens irritated Eddie.

"Shut up," Eddie said.

"*You're* in a good mood," Gary said. "What's eating you?"

"Darrin caught me up there yesterday. He and Mack and Richard got me in the shack."

"You're kidding! Really? How come you're still alive?"

Eddie shrugged. "I got mad, and when they finally let me go, I sicced the dragon on Darrin."

"So?"

"So, maybe it's my fault." He jerked his head at the hillside.

"You think the dragon could've burned down the hill?" Gary asked.

Reluctantly, Eddie nodded.

They stood there a moment in awed silence. A still burning stump flamed up like a gas burner just lit. They stared at it until it subsided to a charred, smoking lump again.

"I bet there's nothing left of their hideout," Gary said.

"Just the hole where it was."

"Well, so what? Who's gonna know the dragon did it? You won't get in trouble, Eddie."

"It's dangerous when things get out of control," Eddie said. "It's bad. I feel bad, Gary."

"Ah, come on. It wasn't your fault."

"Yes, it was. The dragon's mine, and I sent him."

Monday morning Miss Clark was back with her foot in a walking cast, but that passed unnoticed in the glare of news about Darrin. Miss Clark's homeroom buzzed with talk about how he'd been picked up by the police. The fire had damaged the old lady's picket fence and threatened her house. In turn, she'd identified Darrin as the boy she'd seen running out of the woods Saturday evening. The sheriff's daughter told a tight group of listeners, gathered around her desk, that not only was Darrin being charged with setting the fire, but his parents had refused to accept responsibility for his good behavior and had left him in jail. They'd told the magistrate Darrin was too wild for them to handle. They'd said he might do better in foster care or a home for boys.

"That can't be true," Eddie muttered to Gary when the sheriff's daughter had finished telling all she knew. "Darrin's parents are nice. They wouldn't be that mean."

"Oh no?" Gary said. "I bet that's just what my father would do if I got in trouble with the law."

Eddie suspected Gary was right about his father. That didn't make it any less horrifying that Darrin's parents, also, would turn against their own son.

Ms. Krantz stopped Eddie in the hall and asked

if he'd done the essay for the contest. "No," he said. "I didn't have the time."

"Too bad," she said and kept going toward the office.

It didn't matter, he thought. He wouldn't have won anyway. He brooded through his classes, seeing pictures in his head of the dead hill, its hide scorched and mutilated. The old lady's house had looked so small and boxy beside its charred fence. Suppose the house had caught on fire and she'd died. He was lucky he hadn't killed someone. And Darrin. How bad could the kid be that his parents wanted to wash their hands of him? Sure he was a hood, but a kid, even if he was a hood, needed somebody who cared about him. Besides, this time Darrin was innocent. He hadn't set the fire. Eddie had, Eddie and his dragon. The woods had been a place for kids to escape to, and now it was gone. Yes, he'd gotten revenge on Darrin all right, but the ashes of his anger filled his mouth.

"I'm giving the dragon back to your father," Eddie told Gary who was sitting beside him on the bus they were taking to the park after school. Mina had an end seat across the aisle.

"You crazy?" Gary asked. "What for?"

"Because I can't control him. I get too mad, and I can't handle him."

"Don't do it. You'll make my father mad. He'll think *you* stole the dragon."

Eddie shook his head stubbornly.

"And you don't know for sure," Gary lowered his voice to a whisper in case any of the kids on the bus were listening, "that the dragon set the fire. You don't, do you?"

"No," Eddie said. "The fire could've just been an accident, and your father could've just knocked over the lamp by accident, and Miss Clark could've just broken her foot by accident, and Darrin could've busted his finger that time by himself. But how come all those things happened when they did, right when I was mad?"

Gary raised his eyebrows. "It's weird," he admitted.

From across the aisle, Mina piped up, "Besides, I seed him chase your father, Gary."

"The dragon's going back to the store," Eddie said positively.

"Why don't you just heave it in the back of your closet," Gary begged.

Because he didn't trust himself to own a deadly weapon. And because Mina thought she had hurt Tom with the dragon. If Eddie couldn't control his anger, how could he expect his little sister to control her bad temper? No, the dragon was too dangerous. "Because I don't want anything else bad to happen because of me."

"So what are you going to do, just hand it to him and say, 'Here's your dragon back, Mr. Winowski'? That'd go over good. That'd go over *real* good. I bet he'd make me not be your friend no more."

"I know," Mina said. "We can do it like on TV."

"How'd they do it on TV?" Gary asked.

"Well, this girl, she stole a doll from a store, and she wanted to put it back. So her and her friend talked, and this other girl put it back while the store lady wasn't looking. See. Simple." Mina opened her hands palms up to show how simple it was.

"Yeah?" Gary said doubtfully. "So who talks to my father and who puts the dragon back?"

"You and Eddie talk, and I'll put the dragon back," Mina said. "I'm little. He won't see me."

"No," Eddie said.

"Why not?" Gary asked. "It should work, Eddie. Anyways, *you* can't put it back because he'll watch you, and I'm too chicken to do it. Mina's the only one who'd get away with this caper."

They got off the bus at the park, but instead of going on the slide, they sat down to plan what they could talk to Mr. Winowski about that would keep him occupied. When they'd finished planning, Eddie took the shoe box out of the backpack and unwrapped the dragon. All three sat on the bench in the playground looking at it. Finally, Mina reached over and touched the dragon's head with the tip of her finger. "Bye," she said. "I hope you get a good home."

Eddie's eyes blurred. He was going to miss his blue-winged beauty, his pet, protector, comforter at night. And it hadn't been the dragon's fault ever. It was his. If only he didn't get so furious and frustrated. The thing was, being handicapped made him an easy victim. If he had muscles that worked, he could defend himself. It was being so helpless that made him explosive.

Stop it, he told himself. Deliberately, he did what he usually did when he felt sorry for himself. He thought about all the ways he had of enjoying life: through sights and sounds and smells, through thinking and reading and loving. You're lucky, Eddie, he reminded himself. You're lucky in lots of ways. The fire had been terrible, and he deserved to be punished for causing it. Giving up his dragon was the punishment.

For once Mr. Winowski was smiling. He was helping a lady fit a fancy carved wooden chair into the trunk of her car. He kept smiling even after she'd driven off, and he noticed the three of them standing there in his doorway.

"What are you doing here, Gary? I told you you could have the afternoon off."

"Eddie and me wanted to talk to you," Gary said.

"What about?"

"Ah—" Gary looked at Eddie anxiously. "You tell him, Eddie."

"Yeah, sure," Eddie said. "If ah, if I could cover for Gary so he could go out for football next fall—" Eddie began. Face to face with Mr. Winowski, he was nervous. What they'd planned to say sounded silly considering how Mr. Winowski felt about him.

"What'da ya mean, cover for him? In the store? Football? Gary, you want to play football?"

"Yeah, Dad. I told you. I'm really good at football, and if I could practice, you know."

His father studied him, his eyes behind the thick glasses going to his son's broad shoulders. "You're too dumb to be a quarterback."

"I'd be good at tackling and blocking though," Gary said.

"You think so, huh." Mr. Winowski took off his glasses and wiped them, considering.

Mina had disappeared inside, Eddie noticed. He wished they'd discussed where she should leave the dragon, and he hoped she was finding a good hiding place.

"You know," Mr. Winowski said thoughtfully, "when I was in school, I couldn't play anything. I had to get home to take care of my mother every day. She had arthritis so bad she couldn't even get the refrigerator door open." He gave Gary another long look. "So you want to play football?"

"Yeah," Gary said.

"How come you never told me before?"

"I did tell you," Gary said.

Eddie's eyes didn't leave Mr. Winowski's face. He was afraid if he looked for Mina, Mr. Winowski would notice she was gone.

"I used to like football myself. I could've played it

if I'd had a chance. Yeah, well, we'll see," Mr. Winowski said. "You do good this summer, and maybe come fall, we'll work something out." He looked at Eddie. "Not with him though. I gotta have somebody can talk to the customers so they understand. No offense," Mr. Winowski said mildly to Eddie.

Eddie smiled. That apology was as close as Mr. Winowski had ever come to being nice to him. "I'm talking better," he said. "Most of the time people get what I say."

Mr. Winowski nodded. "Yeah. Okay," he conceded. "But you're not ready to cover for Gary in the store yet."

Mina's hand stole into Eddie's. Mr. Winowski glanced down at her suspiciously. "Where were you? Did you go in that store by yourself?"

She looked at him wide-eyed, then hid her face against Eddie's arm as if she were shy. The instant shyness amazed Eddie, who'd never seen her act that way before.

"Mina's a good girl," Gary said. "She's a real cute kid, Dad."

"Okay, okay." Mr. Winowski sounded weary, worn out maybe from being fairly good-natured for so long. "You want to help me move those boxes out of the back now you're here, Gary?"

"Sure, Pop." Gary winked at Eddie. They'd pulled it off. They were home free.

Quietly, Eddie and Mina began the long walk

home. "I didn't lie when he asked me, did I, Eddie?"

"No," he said, finally understanding the point of her sudden shyness. "No, you didn't."

"But I don't like that man."

"Me either."

"And I wish we didn't leave our dragon there."

"Where did you leave it?" Eddie asked.

"I hid him under some papers by the machine that the money goes in."

"Yeah," Eddie said. "Good. Maybe Mr. Winowski'll think the dragon was there all this time."

At least he didn't have to worry about paying the fifteen dollars anymore, Eddie thought, and he could stop feeling guilty now that he'd punished himself. So for a change, he didn't have any problems in his life. He should feel fine. Except he didn't.

"Hey, Mina," he said, wanting to thank her for her help. "You know you're a great little sister?"

"I know," she said. As usual, her self-confidence made him laugh.

In his dream that night, the dragon was searching for him, its blue wings invisible against the inky sky, its eyes gleaming like red stars amidst the white. In his dream, Eddie felt sad right down to his knuckle bones. He felt as if he were missing part of himself.

II

The Contest

Darrin wasn't in school the next couple of days. Feeling guilty that Darrin was sitting in jail because of something the dragon had done, Eddie asked Richard how he was doing.

"He's coming back tomorrow," Richard said, "and you better watch out."

"How come?"

"'Cause Darrin doesn't like you."

"That's okay," Eddie said, relieved that things were normal again. "I don't like him either."

Anita told Eddie she'd heard that Darrin had begged his parents not to send him away, and they'd agreed to give him another chance. His punishment for starting the fire was that he had to pay for the old lady's fence and take care of her yard all summer.

"But he *didn't* start the fire," Eddie said.

"Well, he says he did," Anita said. "See, they were cooking hot dogs, and he left the fire burning when he went home, and the wind came up and spread it." She'd gotten her information from the sheriff's daughter.

Eddie didn't know what to think. If it *had* been Darrin who started the fire, the dragon was innocent, and Eddie shouldn't have banished it to The Treasure Shop. He wondered if Mr. Winowski had found it under the papers next to the cash register yet. Somebody could already have come in and bought it. Magic or not, it was worth fifteen dollars.

"Gare," Eddie asked at lunch, "how's the dragon doing?"

"It's hanging in the window again," Gary said. "Why?"

"Just asking."

After he'd finished eating, Eddie went to the library to return a book on Lou Gehrig that was due. "How'd the contest come out, Ms. Kranz?" he asked.

"Nobody's won yet," she said. "Didn't you hear the announcement about extending the deadline? It's tomorrow now. And we changed the rules. The three finalists will all read their pieces to the assembly Friday, and the winner will be chosen by popular vote." Ms. Kranz smiled at Eddie. "You'd have a good chance, Eddie. Kids really like you."

"They do?"

"Sure they do. Haven't you noticed?"

He thought about it. It was true kids smiled at him often and greeted him by name, kids he didn't even know. "Did you get a lot of essays?" he asked Ms. Kranz.

"No, just a handful. That's why we extended the deadline. The library club meets tonight, and I've got to make them write something."

In his mind Eddie saw his dragon dangling sadly from a hook in Mr. Winowski's dingy store window. "Maybe I'll give it another try," he said. "I almost wrote something, but it didn't turn out."

"Try again tonight," Ms. Kranz said. "You can do it. I know you can." She winked at him.

They were running the six hundred in gym that afternoon. Without being asked, the substitute gym teacher excused Eddie. Since he felt tired and needed the time to think about his essay, he didn't object. He settled down in the shade of the tree next to the parking lot to watch the others.

A few minutes later, a girl on the steps of the school yelled to him. "Eddie, Miss Clark wants to see you."

"What for?"

"I don't know. She's marking compositions in her room."

Uh-oh, he thought. What now? Today Miss Clark had assigned them to write about what they wanted to do in life. He'd explained why he wanted to be a psychologist. Maybe he'd spelled psychologist wrong, and she was going to make him write it twenty times on the blackboard. It'd be just like Miss Clark to drag him indoors on a beautiful spring day for something like that. She could probably see him from her window, taking it easy under the tree.

When he entered her room, Miss Clark looked up and smiled at him. She put her red marking pen down on the stack of compositions and motioned him toward the seat in front of her desk. He sat, preparing to get yelled at despite her smile.

"I saw you all by your lonesome out there," she said, "and thought this might be a good time for us to talk. First of all, I want to say I was touched when the art teacher told me how upset you were to hear about my foot. You're a nice boy, Eddie, and I think I understand how important it is to you to be like normal kids despite your—well, you know."

"Yeah, I know," Eddie said. He suspected she was being nice now because she thought he liked her. He was tempted to set her straight on that, especially since it galled him that she didn't think he was normal. And why couldn't she say the word "disability" out loud? Was there something shameful about being disabled? Probably to her there was.

". . . But it's also important to be realistic," Miss Clark continued. "What I mean is—well, are you really serious about wanting to become a psychologist?"

"Sure, I am."

"Do you realize that a psychologist needs not only a college degree, but maybe even a PhD?"

"Well," he said, "I could try to get a scholarship."

"But, Eddie, even if you did manage the education, how would you get a job?"

"By applying for one."

"What?" she asked. When he'd repeated himself, she sighed. "For a psychologist, communication is very important. Your speech would count against you."

"My speech?"

"You don't speak clearly," she said gently.

Gentle or not, she was going too far. "I'm talking better all the time." He stood up in his agitation. "You should have heard me in first grade. I bet I'll speak as good as you before I'm out of college."

"I'm sure you'll *try*." Her smile was sympathetic. "But you ought to think about what else you'd be good at that wouldn't—"

"I'd better get back to my gym class," he interrupted her to say. It was urgent that he get out of her room before he exploded and said something bad.

She looked annoyed at being cut short, but she excused him, returning to her marking as he seesawed out of the room. Just then the bell rang for next period. Eddie squeezed his weak hand with his good one, wishing he had something to sock. Mina's kindergarten teacher had told her to sock her pillow instead of a person when she got mad. Eddie wished he had a pillow handy.

Gary burst into the cool hallway, his tee shirt sweaty from running. "Where'd you go, Eddie?"

"Miss Clark called me in to tell me I'm not going to make it as a psychologist."

"How come?"

"Because I can't talk right."

"You tell her off?" Gary asked and headed for the locker room. Eddie trailed behind him.

"Gare," Eddie said. "You know what I'm going to do?"

"Put a tack on her chair?" Gary joked.

"No, I'm going to show her. I'm going to prove she's wrong."

"Good," Gary said. "How?"

"I'm going to win that library contest."

"Uh-oh," Gary said.

"What's the matter? Don't you think I can do it?"

"I don't know. I hope you do though." He held out his damp, dirty hand and Eddie shook it. "Luck," Gary said as if he expected Eddie would need a pile of it.

The composition took twelve sheets of spiral notebook paper. Eleven ended in the wastebasket.

blond hair and kicking her heel against the rung of her chair. She looked terrified. To his right was the fourth grade boy who was supposed to be a genius. Eddie felt like a senior citizen, being the only sixth grader. The genius was holding a typed wad of paper, thick as a book. Eddie's page was smudgy now and wrinkled. He wished the whole thing was done. He'd been crazy to think he could win.

Half an hour passed before the three contestants had their turn. Good thing they'd been given chairs, Eddie thought.

"Ladies first," the principal said and nodded his silver head at the tiny girl next to Eddie.

She popped to her feet and stepped forward clutching her paper. It was hard to understand her, even though Eddie was sitting behind her, because her voice was so soft. When she'd finished, she heaved a sigh of relief and turned her back on the spatter of applause, rushing back to her seat. Eddie hoped he'd be next. He wanted badly to get it over with, but no such luck. The brain got the nod from the principal, probably because he was younger than Eddie.

The brain had a big voice. It boomed out about how great books were and how all the knowledge man had was to be found in them, so that every generation could build on what the last generation and all those before it had come up with. Books allowed man to build knowledge like a pyramid including all the contributions of the past.

"Without books we'd still be in caves because no generation could invent everything alone," the brain said. "Take architecture . . ." He took architecture through a long explanation of all you had to know to make a skyscraper that wouldn't collapse of its own weight. Hadn't the kid learned how to summarize yet, Eddie thought. Listening for so long was making his mind glaze over.

"Now take food production," the brain continued. When he turned another page, a few groans came from the audience. However, they clapped enthusiastically after he'd finished, maybe *because* he'd finished, Eddie thought. Not that the kid didn't deserve credit for being thorough.

"Your turn, Eddie," the principal said.

He was stiff from sitting so long, but he smiled gamely as he stepped up to the microphone. "Hey, listen," he said. "Mine's real short." They all laughed. "But you're going to have to listen hard, because I don't speak that clearly. Okay?"

"Okay," a few voices called back amiably.

He looked at Mina who was staring at him, as wide-eyed with terror as if she were the one on the platform. Confidently, he held his hand up. "Here goes," he said. "Ahem."

He made himself go slow and give every word its due. He didn't have to do more than glance at the paper because he'd memorized his paragraphs from having gone over them so much in the library.

"About books and me," he said. "That's the title, kind of basic, but it does the job, right?"

"Right," they called back.

"Okay, now." He held up his hand for silence again. They quieted immediately. That made him feel good. "Books and me, we're friends," he said. "Now I've got other friends. There's Gary. He's my best friend. And my little sister Mina, she's my best buddy in the family, and I have to admit sometimes, just sometimes, when I'm really tired and something funny's on TV, the TV set is my friend. But as friends go, the TV set's just an acquaintance. I take my real problems to the library for solutions. Like how to earn money. There's a book on that subject, believe it or not. And if I need someone to talk to me, all I do is pick up a book. I find good company there.

"Another thing, when I'm in a book, nothing bothers me. I'm really in it, or maybe out of it, if you know what I mean."

The laughter reassured him. *Some* of them must be understanding him.

Hopefully he continued. "Now I'm a slow sort of guy. You've all seen me walk down the hall; so you know that. And lots of times people don't have patience enough to let me finish what I want to say, but when I read a book, boy, am I fast. Just call me Speedy, when I read a book.

"That's why I say that next to Gary and Mina,

books are my best friends. . . . Well, that's it. Thanks for listening." He smiled and took a step backward.

The silence lasted a second too long. They hadn't gotten it, Eddie thought. They'd just been polite. Or maybe they'd understood and thought his speech was stupid. He ducked his head in embarrassment, feeling nearly as bad as when he'd wet his pants in the woods.

Then all of a sudden the clapping began. Once it started, kids went wild and began yelling, "Yay, Eddie! Way to go!" It took the principal to calm them. Mina's face began to brighten. It brightened until she was beaming.

The vote was by show of hands. It didn't take very long to count the hands for the small girl or for the brain, and so many hands went up for Eddie that there wasn't any need to count them to tell he'd won.

He accepted his prize money in such a daze that he didn't remember receiving it. In the hall on the way to class, Darrin passed him and gave him a whack on the back that was slightly harder than comfortable. "Hey, Speedy," Darrin said. "Good speech."

Eddie gulped in amazement.

"Speedy," Eddie was called twice more on the way to the bus.

"I think you got a new nickname," Gary said.

"Could be a lot worse," Eddie told him. "Listen, Gare, can you lend me five bucks? With the ten I just won, I've got enough to pay for the dragon. I'll pay you back tomorrow."

Gary nodded and asked with a grin, "You sure that's what you want to blow your prize money on?"

"Yeah," Eddie said. A small hand slipped into his. "That okay with you, Mina?" he asked. "If I buy the dragon back?"

"Uh-huh," she agreed, and she added, "I was proud of you, Eddie."

"Thanks. I was proud of me too."

Eddie felt powerful. He felt strong, strong enough to fight his own battles without any help from magic dragons. But they'd been through some pretty tricky experiences, he and his pet, and Eddie was grateful. Trying to control the dragon had taught him much about anger and revenge. Besides, he and the dragon were bound together now, and he longed to see those delicate blue wings shining in the sunlight, and to hear the dragon's contented purr as it nestled its silky head against his shoulder at night.

"Come on, you guys, hurry," Eddie told Mina and Gary. "We have to rescue my dragon from The Treasure Shop."

"You're weird, Eddie," Gary said. "You know you're weird, you and that dragon?"

"Weird!" Eddie protested. "What's the matter with you, Gary? Can't you tell the difference between weird and wonderful?"

"All right, you're weird," Gary said. "And the dragon's wonderful."

"Now you got it," Eddie said happily. "That's about right."

He hauled himself up the high step of the bus behind Gary and Mina, confident that he was making progress speedily in the right direction.